Depen

For Pagley,

for my friends J & C
and for A

In memoriam Stevie

DEPENDENCE DAY

by

Robert Newman

ARROW

This edition first published by Arrow Books Limited 1995

1 3 5 7 9 10 8 6 4 2

First published in the United Kingdom in 1994 by
Century
Random House UK Ltd,
20 Vauxhall Bridge Road, London SW1V 2SA

Arrow Books Ltd
Random House UK Ltd,
20 Vauxhall Bridge Road, London SW1V 2SA

Random House Australia (Pty) Limited
20 Alfred Street, Milsons Point, Sydney,
New South Wales 2061, Australia

Random House New Zealand Limited
18 Poland Road, Glenfield
Auckland 10, New Zealand

Random House South Africa (Pty) Limited
PO Box 337, Bergvlei, South Africa

Random House UK Limited Reg. No. 954009

A CIP catalogue record for this book is available from the British Library

Papers used by Random House UK Limited are natural, recyclable products
made from wood grown in sustainable forests.
The manufacturing processes conform to the environmental regulations of the
country of origin.

ISBN 0 09 9 948231 2

Filmset by SX Composing Ltd, Rayleigh, Essex
Printed and bound in Great Britain by
Cox & Wyman Ltd, Reading, Berks.

CONTENTS ─────────────────────

ACKNOWLEDGEMENTS

The author wishes to thank James Parker, Jon Thoday, Kate Parkin, James Herring, Martine McDonagh, Steffi and Lenny Kaye, my Huckleberry friend, Jonathan and Jane, Dolly Kerr, Gavin Hills, Wilbur Sanders, Jeff and Lynn Wood, Bill Tennant, James Midgley, James astor, the "M", Chris Roberts and R. Geralt Jones and family.

PRELUDE

FAN WORSHIP _____

'Would the heavens have fallen if I had rendered Kurtz that justice? But I couldn't. I could not tell her. It would have been too dark – too dark altogether . . .'

Marlowe ceased and sat apart, indistinct and silent in the pose of a meditating Buddha. Nobody moved for a time.

'We have lost the first of the ebb,' said the Captain suddenly, switching the light on. We all smiled polite yes-we've-been-listening faces at Marlowe, but the fact was that his big anecdote had bombed. Everyone was totally bummed out. So much so that the sea-reach of the Thames, which before had looked like a tranquil waterway, now seemed to me to lead to the heart of an immense darkness (I remember thinking).

The silence fell again, as thick and dark as the bank of black cloud barring the offing. Resignedly, I felt it incumbent upon me to save the evening. I had morale on the *Nellie* to think of as well.

'Did I ever tell you my David Bowie story?'

Sixty seconds' pell-mell and the crew were hunkered round with coffee, munchies and duty-free Capstans.

'This all happened about three or four years ago. I

don't know if you've met my friend Colin Liddle. If you didn't know Colin, you'd think he looked a bit boring, 'cos he wears like sensible shoes, a deal of green C&A jumper, and one of those blue woollen hiker jackets that German tourists are murdered in. I've known him since school. If we met now, we wouldn't have anything in common, but, you know, we grew up together, and so there's that sense that there's some understanding which might transcend the fact of having nothing to talk about.

'OK, so Colin's walking past this theatre, the audience are all jabbering out into the evening, and *BOOM!* – there's David Bowie. In the flesh. The eyes, everything. Colin goes up to him, opening his briefcase, one of those *Joe 90* ones – '

'Attaché.'

A weary pause.

'Yes. Thank you, Marlowe. An *attaché* case, everybody . . . And Colin says, "Look, I'm sorry to hassle you, you must get really tired of this, but could I have your autograph? And if you could also sign this card, that'd be brilliant, 'cos it's for my girlfriend's birthday party tomorrow."

'Bowie turns to him, very polite and open.

'"Of course. No trouble at all," he says in that surprisingly Brixton voice – a South London John Hurt. "What's her name?" His spoken voice lets you imagine how fate might have swapped him and, say, Joe Brown or Adam Faith – how Bowie might have been that other type of all-rounder: panto and soft TV all-rounder, chirpy face and bitter regret all-rounder.

'"Oh, could you just put, 'To Jackie'?"

10

'Bowie, head down, Colin's office Pentel in his Bowie hand, writes, "Happy . . . birthday . . . for . . . tomorrow." Colin puts the card back in his case, glad all over.

'"Thanks. OK, don't worry, I won't bother you anymore. Ha ha," he says, balancing the open case on his knee, raised like a curtsy.

'"Not at all," says Bowie, hands behind back in an ankle-length mac. Cocking his head towards Colin, he asks, "Which way are you walking?"

'"I'm going up Upper Street."

'"So am I," he smiles. They walk off together and presently come to a corner.

'"Oh well, here's me," says Colin, "It's great meeting you . . . Wow, I just can't believe how normal you are."

'Bowie stands there, suddenly touched, like rooted to the spot.

'*"Thank you."*

'Colin walks away, swinging his case down the road. A bit of a story to tell. Not much, but, you know, still better than Marlowe's . . .' This got big laughs from the crew of the *Nellie*. 'That night Colin and one of his dull mates are leaving the Mixer. Fighting their way out through the loud smoke. "'Scuse me, excuse me please, 'scuse me . . ." They pause for someone to take a pool shot; someone else huffs before getting out their way, like they might just stand there all night until he goes to the john. ". . . Excuse me, ta." And Colin's out in the quiet night air.

'"David Bowie!"

Turning round, baring *those* teeth (two front retractors), in *that* smile. "What a coincidence!"

11

'"Which way are you going?"

'"I'm just going up the Holloway Road," said Bowie, taking a step that way. Colin motioned that, regretfully, he was going the other way. "I mean, *down* it," Bowie smiled quickly.

'They came to a corner again.

'"Well, what a day! See you, er, David."

'David Bowie grabbed Colin's arms at the elbow, stared deep into his soul. Then he turned and walked away. At the traffic island, a lorry obscured him a second, and when it had passed he'd vanished.

'Next morning, Colin staggered down from bed and opened the front door to take the milk in. David Bowie was asleep on his doorstep. Ever so quietly he closed the door again, and went back inside. By midday, he dared glimpse through goose-pimpled bathroom window, and saw no human shape below. David Bowie had left the building.'

The coffee jug was spluttering on empty, burning off the last brown bubbles and blisters. My audience – rapt – hadn't noticed, but it was beginning to bug my concentration. I killed the Calor Gas. Trundle trundle trundle: from his dark corner Polish Joe rolled in a full bottle of Bailey's. Hoy-day! We all held out sleeve-wiped coffee mugs.

'Cheers gentlemen . . . That evening, Colin stepped out, Piat D'or in a Budgen bag, a botch of wrapping-paper under his arm and that triple-score birthday card. He was still in that state of mind where you think if you stick to the path of your old life, the new invading voodoo won't last. You'll see it off – '

'*That's* what I was trying to *say*!' cried Marlowe. He

shook his head, smiling ruefully, like someone who's told the answer to a simple crossword clue that's had them stumped. (A smile not unlike Kurtz's final one come to think of it. Something had become very important to Kurtz in those last days. Something Kurtz had had to find out if it was the last thing he did. 'May be found in the Hammer House . . . two words – 3, 7.')

'Colin checked at the front door. An empty street. He stepped out. "Hello Colin," said an android voice. Check again.

'In the back of a grey limo, the Thin White Duke wore a party hat, had Donald Pleasance eyes. "What a coincidence. Do you want a lift to Jackie's party?" Bowie got out to hold the car door open. He was wearing sensible shoes, green C&A jumper, and that type of blue woollen hiker jacket that German tourists are murdered in. He hugged Colin to him like he needed Colin's lungs to breathe. "Oh! I've really missed you," cried Bowie. "We mustn't be apart again. If ever a whole day went by and I didn't talk to you, I'd kill myself."

'David Bowie took out a black-handled bread-knife, staring past Colin. "If ever I thought your parents had been cruel to you Colin . . ." He stabbed the air six times, miming Mr and Mrs Liddle's execution, losing himself in the role (unusually). "You're the only person that cares. You're the only one that really sees. My parents don't; my friends are so immature. I won't get in the way of your life. God, that's the last thing I want! Just let me be part of it."

'"Er, I'm not going to the party, I feel a bit tense."

'"Has someone been nasty to you, Colin? Where do

they live?" Bowie stabbed the air ten times more with his bread-knife. Underarm at first, then, when under-arm wasn't enough, thrashing out all over, ripping the air.

'"No, I'm not going to the party – see you."

'An hour later Colin snuck out the back. He took the VCR raiders' way out: over his back wall into the bin-bag alley. He side-stepped a stack of rain-soaked catalogues, some broken glass, and . . . (what else do they have in these places? It's been such a long time, my dears) . . . and a dead kangaroo.

'He didn't come back until merry dawn, Mr Happy Reveller. His footsteps loud in the curtained shell of his street. You feel safe at that time of the night: safe in the knowledge that bad guys need their sleep too. He slowed up – on edge. No rogue limo, nobody. But for some reason he had that sinking feeling.

'Up above, red and yellow clouds lay swollen and bruised, as if, thought Colin, Bowie had been up all through the night stabbing the air far and wide with his bread-knife. Far and wide and like he'd never stop. And so Colin was kind of already prepared for the next thing . . .

'"You lied to me. I trusted you and you let me down."

'"You better come in. I think we need to talk."

'Bowie got up from the night-coloured tiny front-garden mud, where he'd crouched for hours with a garden gnome's silent fixity of purpose.

───────────

Ha ha ha, hee hee hee . . . And you can't catch me.

'Colin Liddle and David Bowie sat in armchairs, face to face, Colin's four-foot record collection running along the floor between them. Two cups of tea. A fired-up electric heater (tiled into the wall). Colin spoke slowly with his head down: "It isn't you I love – it's your music, your albums. Well, quite like . . ." Colin looked up.

'To his dismay Bowie was wearing the cover of *Space Oddity* tied round his head as a mask. The mask had two eye-holes poked through the eyes in the photo. (It's that actual-size photo with the orange spikey hair.) Worse, he was smoking a cigarette through a mouth-hole in the mask. "I don't see the distinction," he replied, holding the Gitanes elegantly in an attempt to appear nonplussed, an attempt scuppered only by wearing an album sleeve on his face. "*Why* can't we be friends? It's because I've only got one eye, isn't it? Is it the Hitler thing? I was waving, I tell you: 'Hello!' Look – see? It's easily done . . . 'Hellooo! Hellooo, Mick!' I mean, I love black people. How can I prove it to you? I'd happily marry a black woman. They're lovely girls, *lovely*. Ah, *that's* why you think we can't be close friends: you think I'm gay. Ha ha! No, no I'm not. There was that dress thing, but I was on drugs and it was like a laugh, ha ha. And anyway, I'm not gay now. I just went through a funny phase . . . But, but – yeah, that's how I know for sure that I'm truly, truly heterosexual . . ."

'The Bowies turned their head as if looking around for the new line of argument. Colin read the "C.L." he'd written in blue biro on the top-right-hand corner of the album sleeve.

'"Or is it because you think I'm too pretentious? Shit, Colin, I could be in a band with good ol' boys playing R 'n' B if you want, and enjoy it too. And with a ghastly name. I dunno – The Hog Dog Foot Stompers, The Steel Mechanism, Copper Engine, or something . . . I'll think of something . . ."

'"You mustn't get the artist, the public persona, confused with the real person," said Colin. "I mean, I like you – but I also like, you know . . ." he glances down at his row of albums, ". . . the fucking Shamen. I – "

'"*Two* eyes! Mr Two Eyes C."

'"I love your work and that, but I don't know who you are." Big breath. "I'm actually on edge when you're around. To put it, you know, honestly, totally honestly – I don't think I'd like you at all if I met you as *you*."

'A few seconds passed. Colin raised his head. In the circumstances, it was – you'll appreciate – difficult to gauge much from David Bowie's facial expression. But then, from out of the eye-holes, twin tears rolled down the front of the buckled *Space Oddity* cover. For a moment it looked as if the photo itself was crying like Our Lady of Lourdes with a pilgrim.

'"Oh God, look, don't cry. I mean, I don't know, I might not . . . We'll never know."

'Colin didn't tell anyone; he was a head-down kind of a guy. There was this one time, looking back – but we all thought it was just a wizard wheeze. It was one lunchtime in Charlotte Street, Jackie suddenly shouted, "Hey, there's David Bowie!" And Colin went, "Oh God, hide me!" but with that passionate intensity of The Bi-annual Great Sarcastic Gag. There was even a rare – for Colin – physical embellishment. Tucked behind Jackie, he was bobbing and stooping, but again totally straight-faced. You know, we thought it was a joke. And like all gags which become mythic among your friends, it had a subtext of "we're so cool that the World's Big Things are mere food for our jape sessions". We just thought he'd excelled himself.

'He felt that if he didn't tell anyone, then only _he_ was affected but the world stayed normal; but if he told someone else then somehow the weirdness, the threat, the oddness, would spread over everything.'

Marlowe nodded earnestly. 'It would have been too dark – too dark altogether.'

'Work kept him sorted. Its detailed tedium saved him: the Vendpac tea he could never finish and which always burnt his fingers; the draught on his back when the double-doors were open for loading; his supervisor yelling at him over the din of machines:

'"This is Andrew, Colin. If you could just show him this floor: ground floor prexels, lock-offs, slidings, and where everything is . . ."

'"A'reet?" said Andrew, a greybeard hippy northerner – Sheffield Wednesday or Leeds, probably.

'Colin nodded but didn't say hello. "OK, this is the bolt-stripper . . . that, um, the iron shavings come out of, and you've got to be careful of . . ."

17

'The northern apprentice stared at Colin, pulled down his beard and put his mouth to Colin's ear.

'"Scary monsters . . ."

'*"WAAAH!"* Colin fell into the sliding bracket machine=thing for turning human hands to blood. He span off, got up, and stood, silently bowing and bowing over his mashed and pulpy hand, appeasing an Asian God of Pain.

'"Oh no, I've hurt you . . ."

'"Piss off out of my life, David Bowie!"

'On hearing this last remark, several colleagues took a moment's pause from their work. They saw a sobbing trainee run out holding a joke-shop beard.

'Bless his heart, he still didn't tell anyone. He told the cops, but not us. "If Mr Jones were to phone again after a complaint had been made," said the WPC, "we would be able to proceed with a caution." She left. The phone rang. Colin picked it up. Away down the line he could hear "Heroes" playing in the background of whatever pad or pen, broken-into slaughter yard, Seventh Day Adventist Church or technicolour pond Bowie was calling out of.

'"Why did you call the police, Colin? Why? Why do you have to torture the one person who loves you? Jackie and Robert don't love you; they're scum. If you don't pick up the phone I'll kill myself. I know you're there. I got a Tarkovsky video out last night, and I pretended we were discussing it afterwards. You were very clever about it . . . I'm still here . . . Hello? . . . I know you're there . . . Why did you do that to me, Colin? Why did you do that? . . . You're a fake and a phoney, and I hope you die in hell. You're just like all the others. FUCK OFF, YOU CUUUNT!!"

'Colin stood there, holding the dead-tone receiver, for an hour in the loneliest listening-booth in the world.

'Next day I'm round his house. One of those rainy-out-cosy-in-misted-up-window-Manor-House-cake-ITV-Seven afternoons. Colin's upstairs so I get the door for him.

'"I've come to read the meter."

'I never like it when officials are younger than me. This young Indian, twenty-two-ish, took off his wet LEB cap off a second. Hair was all temple-to-temple tramlines, zig-zag fades. He put his cap back on and found the box.

'Colin came back down holding a bottle of milk and a paper. He saw the back of a blue LEB coat and cap busy in the cupboard under the stairs. "Who's that?"

'"He's come to read the meter."

'Crouching down in the white-panelled wooden cubby, the meter-man was a-humming and a-whistling to himself and nobody in particular:

"... La-la ... lada de ... take your protein pills and put your helmet on, 10 ... Ground Control to Major Tom ... 7 ... 6 ..."

'*KADABANG!* Colin smashes a full bottle of milk on the closet bhangramuffin's head.

'"*AARGHURGH!*" the Indian kid screams. "Take the money, please! Take the money! Oh God."

'I'm on my feet shouting, "What the fuck are you doing? What are you doing?" – holding Colin off.

'"What's going on?" the meter man's a-screeching, still in the crash position, wincing up at Colin through his elbows. He wants to inspect the bleeding wound,

19

but daren't take his eyes off the mild-mannered maniac.

'"I'm sorry," says Colin.

'Me and the Indian both look at him like "yes . . .?"

'"I thought you were David Bowie, that's all."'

I ceased and lay apart, indistinct and silent in the pose of the Death of Chatterton. Nobody moved for a time.

'We'll just catch the second ebb,' said the Captain gently. I raised my head. High up, searing white streamers of coral cloud promised an Invisible Maypole. In the offing, sea and sky were welded together without a joint. The dancing Thames stretched before us into a luminous haze, like the beginning of a glittering waterway leading to the uttermost ends of the earth.

Someone cranked up the system and the disco boat was off.

BOOK I

One
THE ROSE COTTAGE _____

Nine o'clock and the pub is crowded.

'You notice it's called "Cottage", not the Crown, or the Rose or the "Cock". I'll tell you why . . .'

Behind the bar, a fifty-year-old woman is talking to a first-time punter. She has a handsome, strong face and a gentle smile while she talks. She is wearing a black skirt and a smart, shiny metallic silvery-grey top over her full chest. She has what appears to be a purely ceremonial function, as her grown-up sons and daughters work the busy pumps, taking the next order before going to the till for the change from the last.

'I have a sister who's a Mother Superior over in Ireland, in Mayo. Now, she'd never talk to me again if she knew I ran a pub. So this way she can write to me, and all she knows is that I live in Rose Cottage. Rose Cottage, Arkness, it says on the envelope.'

The punter turns with a packet of crisps in his grin. He holds together half a dozen drinks in one glass cluster.

Buzz is pounding down the cold night street, building up speed, keeping close to the wall. His small head is round, and his body is round like a Bauhaus brick shithouse. Pound. Pound. Pound. His shoulder brushes the wall. With no break in his pounding pace he unfolds the long blade of a Swiss army knife, and puts it back in the swaying hip-pocket of his jacket. He can hear it clink against the loose change in his side-pocket on every other step, like a too-fast military drill instructor: right, right, right-left-right; right, right, clink-chucckk-clink.

The smokey interior. Some recently departed neurotic has torn a beermat into tiny pieces of cardboard on a table which is vacant. On the table's copper surface, a vanished hand, greasy with crisps, has left a palm print, the fingers slightly dragging. Five feet away, Glen stands chatting, smiling. He has blond, straggly thin hair. He looks like a surfer dude. Behind him the circuit-chasing bright colours of the fruit machine wait for money to give them shape and purpose.

Buzz's pounding round the cold outside corner; the Rose Cottage now in view, his mental samples repeating: '*YOU CAN'T LET THAT GO, YOU CAN'T LET THAT GO, YOU CAN'T LET WORD GET OUT THAT HE SAID THAT AND YOU DID NOTHING. HE'S IN TROUBLE NOW. I'M NOT LETTING IT GO. YOU DON'T FUCK WITH ME.*' Right, clink, kerchink, clink, right.

Karen is standing in a group of four, but having drifted out of the conversation is now looking intently at the opening door as Buzz enters and marches fast through the chatting, busy pub.

He headbutts Glen who falls back, splayed against the convex glass front of the fruit machine. Buzz takes the knife from his side-pocket and punches the blade into Glen's stomach just above the belt-buckle, pulling the knife up as high as the Technics logo on Glen's T-shirt chest.

Glen falls down privately; that is to say, there is a strange, anti-climactic understatedness to the way he slips from the fruit machine to the floor. Buzz falls on him. The two of them are down in a quiet thicket made up of wooden table-legs and the undersides of stubby pub-stools. Down here the jukebox and the pub din sound like they're in another room. 'Did I fall down some stairs?' thinks Glen for a moment. Buzz's hand lands on his throat.

Glen is on his back, his head turned to one side, his face an inch away from the balsa-wood underside of a toppled pub-stool. He sees where burgundy velvet is stapled in pleats to the balsa-wood, and a number chalked in the middle. Then something else happens. Something that takes him down, it seems, to yet another room. Only he didn't fall down some stairs to get to this room. Perhaps he was pushed by the side of his head through a brick wall. That's how he got into this further room. For a split second he sees that it is a new and terrifying pain which has thrown his head to the other shoulder. Now, he sees a new-looking white rubber plug in the double wall-socket, and the red top of the switch that's on. The people upstairs have dragged off Buzz. Or perhaps they're about to, or they did ages ago. Glen rolls his eyes up. Heavy boulders, hard to shift. That must be why he's sweaty and breathless. In the black-painted wooden back of the fruit machine he sees perfectly-sawn holes. Perforations of perfect night in the black wood. One perfectly round hole is twice as large as the others. The black-painted wooden back of the machine comes to be everything, and even taps his shoulder with a human hand at one point. But while it has sprouted human hands, he, meanwhile, has swapped places and become the black-painted wooden back of the fruit-machine, with its perfect black holes.

On terra firma, in the upstairs room, punches are thrown. A girl screams. A glass smashes. Did it hit the ground or someone's head? And Buzz is nowhere to be seen. A student vet stems the blood pumping from Glen's gut by pressing the pressure points for a run-over dog.

One evening a few days later, I called for Karen. Three prostitutes stood at the end of her street.

'*YOU WANT SOME PUSSY?*' one roared. I rang Karen's bell, which played a little tune. She came to the door – a shadow, then a colourful impressionist blur, then the woman herself.

'Darling, there are some ladies outside enquiring as to whether we might be in need of any "pussy" this evening.'

'I think we'll be all right.'

'No, we're fine, thanks,' I shouted up to them.

Another pub, another night. Six or seven of us sat at a cluster of small round tables in the Jolly Mower.

'Well, apparently Buzz had sold him some dud E's, and Glen was saying that he wasn't going to pay for them.'

'It was weird – from the minute he walked in I knew what he was going to do. For some reason I was watching right from the moment he walked in, and I saw him and the look on his face and the knife in his hand and I knew he wasn't going to just threaten him with it. I just knew. I wanted to shout out "NO, Buzz!" 'cos I knew what he was going to do, but I was frozen. It was like I was tripping. It just didn't seem real. I was watching him all the way from the door.'

'How do you know him?'

'Well, you just know him, 'cos he's on the scene and a dealer – although I've never bought anything off him, and wouldn't have done anyway. And he always used to come up and ask me out.'

'Yeah, he was dealing next door but one to the cop shop.'

'Did you know Glen?'

'Just to say hi to, you know.'

'No.'

'Did you?'

'No.'

'Are you going to come forward as a witness?'

'No, you know, I don't want to get involved in the whole thing. The police and everything.'

27

'Also you don't know what happened.'

'That's right. 'Cos sometimes when people get stabbed – I'm not saying they deserved it – but sometimes they push their bloody luck, and you think, well, you shouldn't have been such an idiot.'

'Yeah, and the police didn't even cordon the area off, or take names or, like, appeal for witnesses anyway.'

'That's right.'

'What if it had been your sister?' someone said.

MEMO TO MR SCORSESE.

CUT TO THE *NELLIE*, A CRUISING YAWL ON THE THAMES. CAMERA PANS ROUND THE SITTING CIRCLE. IN THE WARM CALOR-LAMP GLOW WE SEE: KAREN DOONAN, KEVIN McSTAY, ROBERT NEWMAN, MARLOWE, POLISH JOE, CLAUD AND THE CAPTAIN.

KAREN: It took three days for Glen to die. He might even have lived . . .

CUT TO HOSPITAL. GLEN LIES THERE WITH TUBES AND MACHINERY. GRAPES IN A CUT-CLASS FRUIT BOWL LIKE A STILL-LIFE. A NURSE IS GIVING HIM A BED-BATH. SHE WASHES HIS COMATOSE,

UNRESPONSIVE HEAD BEHIND HIS EARS.
SHE FEELS A BUMP. HER FINGERS PART
THE STRAW-COLOURED HAIR. A HOLE.

NURSE: Crash!

FLASHBACK.

GLEN ON 'THE ROSE COTTAGE' FLOOR.
THEY ARE RUSHING TO DRAG OFF BUZZ.
DOWN ON THE SCUFFED FLOOR BUZZ
GETS IN ANOTHER UNSEEN STAB. THE
BLADE GOES RIGHT THROUGH THE
SKULL UP TO THE HINGES.

KAREN: (V/O) All the while they'd been stitching
up belly, his brain had been having this massive
haemorrhage.

[And Marty, I don't want you to get into your usual
sentimental catholic tizzy of ambivalence about the
boorish and the criminal, either.]

Sitting on the floor after a pensive fag she phoned the
police after 'Neighbours' and 'Fifteen-to-One', and
two weeks later two policemen knocked on the glass,
chicken-mesh door. Dry sealing plaster flaked off the
pane. She told them what she'd seen.
    Within hours Buzz held Karen's statement in both

hands. By law the defendant has to be shown all statements. He also has the right to know the identity of each witness. But here's the fucked-up thing: the procedure means the defendant sees the actual piece of paper the witness signed. A sheet of paper which has on it the statement, the signatory and the witness's address:

c/o The Amish,
Jeremiah's Barn,
Hiding Under A Big Pile Of Grain,
3 Pitchfork Pokes From The Left.

The next day, however, she went back to college in Nottingham. Here in Nottingham she was untraceable. Here, if things had been different, she might never have known the danger she was in until the danger had passed.

She was a mature student at twenty-six. Since leaving school half-way through the sixth year, she'd worked in record shops, for a concert promoter and in a recording studio. Then she'd taken her A levels in a year, re-taken them the next, and gone to Nottingham.

She had chosen her course badly, opting for Media Studies because that was what she knew. Within minutes of the introductory lecture, she realised that what she wanted was what she didn't know. She wished she'd chosen a more academic course – something with some rigour, shape and structure. Something less like 'Kilroy'. Still, she stuck it out with the thought of changing to Philosophy & Psychology or English or Natural Science next year.

She didn't know she was pregnant until she miscarried. She needed to see her doctor back home. And since she was going to be away from college for a while – so near to the end of year exams – she thought she might as well pack the course in.

It was now a year since Glen's death and the murder still hadn't come to trial. Buzz had murdered Glen while on the run from prison. He'd been on the run for six months. While he was back inside seeing out his last sentence, the police were taking time to make sure that they could get him off the streets for good. Everything was still at stake when word got out to the Arkness she was back.

Karen went at first to stay with her sister Gina in Fallowfields. Gina lived with Maxine as lesbian and lesbian in a terraced house off a quiet speed-bump street. You have to go through an alley to get to their row of terraces. Nos. 106 to 120 are inbetween two roads, a well-kept secret. In every other way this row is exactly the same as every other terrace in the street, or for the next three streets.

Maxine was the more masculine, and yet wore the make-up and the dresses; more radical than Gina, she looked more high-street. She had a laid-back voice, but there was a constriction about her somewhere; a hard face with smooth skin. The more confident and the more withdrawn. There was something decorous in her friendliness, formal in her hospitality. She

worked for the DSS processing claims, and dealing
with claimants whose claims had got lost or turned-
down, refused or delayed.

They had a big dog called Monty. Monty was very
happy to be in an all-female house. He'd been a bat-
tered dog when they found him. Some man must have
done terrible things to him once. If a man walked in,
he'd come and bark and crowd him, obstruct him a bit
without meeting his eye, but you could see in those
wide-open brown eyes that he was terrified. The
temerity of barking at a man cost him a lot. He did it
bravely to honour his hosts, but at the same time out of
fear: a half-arsed attempt to scare away the things that
used to cause him pain.

Maxine sat in a rocking-chair with an inscrutable
expression. Karen sat on the floor, Gina on the couch.

'Maxine's brother got let out,' said Gina with a
chuckle.

'Neil?'

'Yes,' said Maxine. 'About two weeks ago.'

'Where was he?' asked Karen.

'Risley Remand.'

'Yeah,' added Gina, 'and, apparently, he was on the
same floor as Buzz.'

'He was never . . .' said Karen, turning to Maxine.

'Yes,' said Maxine evenly, leaning the rocker forward to pick an empty Rizla packet off the floor.

Gina and Maxine were off on holiday in Ibiza, and
Karen was left alone with the house, where she had its
strange creaks and cupboards to herself.

The phone rang. On Maxine's instructions Karen had not been answering the phone, just leaving the messages to run. It was an unfamiliar male voice on the ansaphone, and Karen carried on walking to the kitchen.

'Hello Karen? Karen, are you there? Hello?' And then impatiently, '*Hello?*'

'Hello?' asked Karen, curiously.

'Oh hi, Karen, it's Neil here. Maxine's brother . . .'

'Oh hi, Neil.'

'I just thought I'd phone and see how you're getting on.'

'Oh fine, thanks.'

'You got everything?'

'Yeah.'

'I was just thinking, why don't you come round seeing as you're all alone in the house?'

Karen was wary now. Neil had never fancied her nor flirted with her before, or even been friendly – and now here he was asking her to come round.

'Thanks, but I think my friend Louise has found us a flat, and so, you know, I'll have to move all my stuff from my old place. Thanks anyway, but I'm not sitting here bored and that,' she said jokily, brightly, chirpily.

'All right,' said Neil, disappointedly. 'All right,' he said, pensively.

Karen lies in the bath of the new flat, her short dyed blonde hair dampened by the steam. Ninety-five per cent of bath-time for her is a hazy, indolent daze. The soaping and rinsing has been got out of the way. Now she is just in to soak. Her upper torso lies above the water-line and has drip-dried half an hour ago, despite being splashed occasionally by palmfuls of bathwater to cool off her red face.

Her reclining breasts have evened out, diffusing at the base towards her armpits. There is a delicate tracery of blue veins, and no strict gradation between nipple, areola and breastage. (A topographer would have been hard pushed to find the demarcation, and would've claimed he needed another day to take some more readings.)

She bestirs herself enough to run her hand over her belly below the ruler-straight water-line. Exactly the same calm belly on the outside, so odd to think of the hormonal high drama raging in her womb. It all feels much calmer now, though. She runs her fingers like a comb through her tidy bush, and tugs the hair up taut to see whether it's time to chop her chuff. Probably, but she can't be bothered, and it may just be the refraction that is making it look a bit Clare Short. She runs a forefinger over the stubble in the fold of her inner thigh. Again, she thinks she probably should – the white plastic razor is on the edge of the bath even – but she can't be bothered. Not now, maybe tomorrow. As yet, she hasn't noticed the silhouette of a man crouched on the ledge outside her frosted-glass window: a dumb show of imminent violence.

She slides back down under the water to cool off her head and wet her hair. She opens her eyes underwater and looks up at the distant-seeming bathroom through the bouncing water-line. She slides up again, running a hand over her face to get the water out of her eyes. A noisy crowbar busts the wooden frame of the window. She screams and leaps from the tub in an upsurge of loud bathwater. The man-shadow jumps away and is gone.

'Louise! Louise!' shouts the naked Karen, sliding a bolt, turning a key. 'Someone's just tried to break in. Shut the windows! Lock all the doors!'

Karen dials 998. She dials 999.

'Someone just tried to break into my house. I don't know if I'm just being paranoid, but I'm a witness in a murder case.'

As she pulled back the curtains next day around noon, the phone – still in the same position on the floor – rang.

'I need to have a word with you,' the familiar voice said.

Next day Karen went round to Gina and Maxine's.

'I went to see my brother,' said Maxine. 'And you know he was in with Buzz? Well, he told me that they've put a contract out on you not to turn up at the trial.'

'Oh no.'

Maxine looked at Gina and went on. Her tone (perhaps to reassure Karen) had an officialness to it, as if what she was saying wasn't shocking. 'I don't know how much it is; or it might just be for a favour owed, because it's a general one – you know, open. Anyone can pick it up.'

'Oh *fuck*. To do what?'

A pause. Then the calm, helpful tone continued: 'He didn't say. I don't know. Maybe five blokes come round, maybe they'll have a gun or something. I mean, they almost certainly wouldn't hurt you at that first meeting anyway, because there wouldn't be any point to it, would there? But I'd move out if I was you. Move out, move away, 'cos the next time they might burn your house down, say. I mean if it's me,' said Maxine, looking over towards Gina, but seeming very calm indeed, 'then at least my stuff's *insured*.'

Karen needed to plan her next move. She went to stay for a couple of nights with her boyfriend Mark, who lived in Stoke. Sitting on the train she had a feeling of being removed from all the other passengers. Outwardly she could still do all the things they could do. She could queue at the buffet just like any other passenger. She could sit with a book and a Walkman on the table; she could read; her eyes met someone else's occasionally and looked away. She could smile at the Asian toddler wandering down the corridor testing a loud 'Allo!' on everyone; she could squeeze past the family crouched in the rubber-mat gap between carriages, their prams and luggage about them. She could still maintain all these outward forms, but some invisible barrier had come down between her and everyone else on the train.

There had, it seemed, been a common connection between her and everyone else, which was only noticeable now that it was gone, now that she was outside it somehow. She couldn't tell what it was exactly, only that she was now not included in something which enveloped everyone else she looked at on the swaying carriage as it swayed over spells of quiet then furious track.

She went and stood in the toilet, not really needing to go. The harshly-lit mirror in the cubicle showed her herself under a more ferocious scrutiny than the human eye. She noticed tiny blonde hairs on her forehead which she'd never seen before, and visible pores on her face at either side of her nose. The maculations in her bluey–green eyes were new to her, too: chips of triangular green and hazel, and lighter bits of blue among the blue.

She crossed the lurching floor. The window was painted-out white. There was only a little eye-level square of transparent glass to look out of. She looked through this at the passing fields, blurry in the short-distance, clear in the long. A large collection of barges in the inlet of a canal went by. The overhead wires of the adjacent, back-to-Wythenshawe track seemed to be the same stretch of wire travelling alongside her peep-hole moving vertically, not horizontally: rising up and falling down in sudden but graceful lifts and drops.

She was no longer one of the passengers looking at each other with vague curiosity. Something harsher and more searching had sought her out and was examining her. This unkind glare had not much interest in her human delineaments; it was trying to see to the very heart of her. The harsh mirror made her think herself a collection of decaying tissue and crude

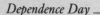

physiology. Was it Evil itself, this force? Or was she already feeling invaded by Buzz's remorselessly sordid and predatory way of looking at the world?

CUT TO *NELLIE*. INT. NIGHT. EVERYONE SITTING ROUND IN THE GENTLY ROCKING BOAT.

KAREN: When I got to Mark's, I phoned Louise 'cos I thought she'd be worried – which she was of course, 'cos I'd just vanished without a trace, and everybody was saying they didn't know where I was and everything. So I called her and I told her about the contract, and I told her not to tell the police, and that I'll be in touch and not to worry, I was OK. She started panicking then and went and told the police.

And I thought if Buzz is trading off his sentence by giving the police the names of a whole series of drug dealers up and down the country – I didn't know he was escaped from prison on the charges he was – and I thought, 'Oh no, I could be in real shit here.'

Until Louise phoned I was going to return home, you see, because everything had been kind of sorted. They knew that I was going to make efforts not to turn up – it had gone back through Maxine – so Louise fucked it all up thru' going to the police. It had come back through Maxine's brother that that

38

was cool as long as I made visible signs, you know, sort of nearer the appropriate time, to be out of the way. A month or two before the case.

The thing is, that would've given me *time* to organise my life, but because of what she did, it meant I had to up and go immediately to show them I was serious. I was really, really angry about that.

———————

She crept into Manchester from Stoke that night. They'd been lucky to get this house from the Housing Association. It was big with a garden. She'd only just moved in.

Karen filled three plastic shopping bags. The phone rang. She jumped. She let it ring. It stopped. This girl, who always took two hours to get ready – bath, hair, clothes, make-up, tea, fag, more make-up for some reason – was out the front door in half an hour. *SLAM!*

'Dearest London . . . are you home of the free or what?' From the inter-city she saw a statue of Old Father Thames, his stone face etched by life and pain, but looking serene and unruffleable despite the green lichen – almost smiling, in a gruff way.

And London said: 'Give me your poor, your sick; give me some of those men in bobble-hats who shout at walls all day, the Dennys and Mad Jacks; give me your overspill-town office boys in Top Man clothes, back to wreak a terrible vengeance for their nine-to-five; give me your smudged vinyl headboards for my DSS B&B's. Give me bagladies pushing knackered prams of significant rubbish. I'll have ten dozen of your scarface tattoo people, and give me this tiny blonde woman holding three over-stuffed carrier bags. Tell her not to be afraid.

'They've all come here, I've seen much worse. Trust me. I mean, look, come through this Euston automatic-door, and now *just look at all these* people. I mean, she's gotta take comfort in that randomness itself, hasn't she? Let me talk to her, while she stands looking left and then right on my crowded pavement. Listen girl, that's quite a tide for any invading voodoo to swim against. Trust me, I'm linked up to the uttermost ends of the earth. I'll look after you. You're safe with me. You're all right. I've done this millions of times. Trust me. Now, er, how much have you got on you?'

Two
AS SHE IS _____

'The very first time I saw your face
I thought of a story, and rushed to reach the end too soon.'

We were leaning against the stern rail of the chugging *Nellie* as those words boomed up from the hold. Kevin was looking through a pack of photos of Svetlana, or Svetlana and him.

'I keep coming back to this one,' he said, dealing me the top one from the shuffled pack. 'This is at Meadowbank Stadium.'

I studied the picture. It is steeped in rich late-afternoon long-shadow sun. Her concentration is gathered, but she's still maybe five or six seconds away from starting her run-up to the (out-of-shot) high-jump bar. For all her face's cool repose, there is something livid there too, like someone having to do something under compulsion, or irritable at the prospect of interruption.

The photo's shot from slightly under. The eye moves up from the track, past her non-denominational trainers and white socks. Not until you've looked at this picture ten times do you notice that her right foot is actually off the ground. Once I saw this, I tried to see it grounded as before but couldn't.

The eye moves up . . .

White high jumper's high thighs going up into the royal blue of those gym-knickers which we've success-fully foisted on women athletes as shorts.

Her torso is serene under the white vest of Romania. A white vest with the yellow and blue sash of a distant grudge, a diagonal division her breasts don't recognise. It runs from above her heart to her right hip.

Her right hip. Her blue shorts. The vast, concrete stadium's whole shadow seeks the triangle of her lap, and, having spent itself there, leaves her left leg out free in the clear sunshine.

Broad, smooth shoulders. Her long white arms – calm by her side – give away nothing of how near she is to take off, except in her right hand: fingers twisted like a Da Vinci detail.

A silver necklace or two. Her black hair is pegged up for business, high on the back of her head like a 1950s ponytail. The mouth wasn't made for the life it had, it never expected to be pressed into service to look quite so determined all the time.

I handed the picture back. The strips of whitewater running in our wake cut a crisp sound from the wavy brown river.

'Throw it in,' I told him.

Three
A LETTER TO
KENNY ROGERS _____

Dear Mr Rogers,

I never realised the emotional content of 'If You Happen To See The Most Beautiful Girl In The World'. I used to think it was just a neat little conceit. But now I know you know.

One of the things about being chucked is that all these songs, which were just songs before, start making sense. It's like they've snapped into focus; suddenly they're speaking directly to me. 'Oh, so *that's* what that song's about, I never realised.'

Me and Svetlana split up. I feel terrible, like someone died. She chucked me.

Did you find – when she 'walked out on you' – that your friends thought you'd want to hear bad things about her? They don't realise you're still in love with her. Even after she's gone the fact remains that she is still the most beautiful girl in the world. Friends, thinking they were helping, would say to me, 'Well, she has been around a bit, though, hasn't she?' Shut up, I'm mourning! If she'd died, would this same friend be picking his way through crematorium wreaths to say to me, 'It's a terrible loss, but if it's any small consolation, she was a right slapper'?

The small congregation files inside the crematorium. The Yamaha organ ends on a soft-pedal minor chord which takes a long time to clear. The vicar speaks.

'As we commit her body to its final resting place, I'm sure we would all like to ask God a question: "Who *hasn't* she shagged?"'

Maybe it's as well we broke up. (I don't believe that for a moment but I'm not turning down any rationalisation!) Maybe it's as well, because in the last weeks before we split, I didn't like the man I was becoming. I remember driving past a Zero Tolerance poster, saying: '50% OF ALL WOMEN WHO ARE MURDERED ARE MURDERED BY A CURRENT OR FORMER PARTNER.' A shocking statistic. But instead of thinking what a vindication of Susan Faludi, or whatever, my only thought when I saw that poster (because this woman was breaking my fucking heart), my only thought was: 'No! Not murdered; not murdered . . . EXECUTED!'

A humiliating fall from my feminist self-image. I think of myself as a feminist ontologically. (Ontologically means I don't have to act like one at any point in time.)

But then it was all humiliating climb-downs. 'Honey, trust me,' I said, 'you're convinced I'm going to hurt you, but I'm not. I'm just gonna make you happy.' And then I slept with Karen. It's true what they say about when the dick is hard the mind is soft. When I was being unfaithful my mind was full of all these excuses, all these good reasons: '. . . Well, it's good for her because it'll take the pressure off her in the relationship, and it'll be good for me 'cos I won't be so hung up on her; it'll be good for my ex-girlfriend because it'll show that I still care about her; and it'll be good for the situation in Sarajevo (the Serbs and the Bosnians, in looking upon my own mindless destruction of something beautiful, may perhaps reflect) . . .'

Is that what the 'tell her I'm sorry' bit is about, Mr Rogers?

One day soon, the 5 a.m. will come when I can think about that night without biting my knuckles over each remembered detail. Here's one.

The car alarm freakishly going off three times for no reason that night. ('The raven himself is hoarse . . .' etc.) I went down three flights of stairs into the rain and open-air, where common-sense might have breathed.

'The electronic siren will pulsate at 120DB and all traffic indicator lights will flash for 30 seconds approx. Then close down and automatically re-set to provide protection against any further attempt.'

The Saab remembered the impression of her sweet arse on its black leather seats. It clung to the last vestige of her smell: Chanel mingled with that vanilla body-lotion stuff. It was fond curator of her relics: Camel butts in its ashtray, her *Definitive Simon & Garfunkel* on the littered rubber floormat, a Bounty wrapper passenger-side. It remembered long journeys over in no time, where the world seemed at one remove. And though it remembered the bitter 200-mile rows, its fine computerised tuning could hear something worthwhile in amongst all the shouting.

And so each time I poured Karen a glass of wine, or looked a pulse too long at her naked belly between skirt and shirt, the wordless alarm squawked. '*Air movement can cause the ultrasonic module to trigger.*'

It detected the shift in the air as lust and sentimentality made their old and shabby collusion. Three times it went off. Three times down the stairs I ran. Three times up the stairs, bounding past the sunken lives of the ground and first floors, to sink life on the third. One big betrayal that changed the direction of everything.

Ah, the Ancient Mariner imagery again, that men are so fond of. If you put everything down to one fateful mistake that took you straight from A to Z, then – amongst the gnashing and wailing – you dodge responsibility for B through to Y. Here *is* where the plot swerved, however. Perhaps not irrevocably – though I have my doubts – but into new waters that I couldn't stomach. And it is tempting to look back now and see it all as one fixed course leading from that sexual betrayal ('You don't understand the enormity of what you've done,' she said), to the last time I shagged the Most Beautiful [Woman] In The World.

Here's where the story ends . . .

In his chapter on love, a great philosopher once wrote 'that we may feel in things immediate and infinitesimal a sure premonition of things ultimate and important. Fine senses vibrate at once to harmonies which it may take a long time to verify . . . Well-bred instinct meets reason half-way, and is prepared for the consonances that may follow.' That's why I could never love a woman who didn't love me coming on her face; who didn't simply love the touch, taste, feel and smell of cum, sperm, spunk or – in sixteenth-century slang – *nature*.

On the silent shifting hotel bed, Svetlana said something to be treasured and I, like a dupe falling for the simplest hypnotic trick again, only just had time to pull out and stagger two steps on my knees, before I came, and she greedily (*greedily!* Oh, God bless her and the Romanian people as a whole! Praise be to the *fervour* of the Orthodox church!) brought me, it, up into her mouth and then out and over her neck and face.

I felt stressed with my haploids lying exposed like that, my 23n all over the place. Belly, breast, hair, pillow-case. An unkind word might kill me now.

Pleased at the good turn-out, however. I'm a once-a-night bod, really, and we'd done it once already. It was in the ten minutes it took to pick her up from her flat. A kiss and then another kiss. She had her coat on, and it was, I'm afraid, the old pornographic contrast of many layers and no layers. (Her canvas jeans dropped not even to the knees.) Oh, and the other erotic constituent, I suppose, was that I once saw an old lady in an almost identical coat killed outright by a lorry. (Only joking, Kenny! 'I've bought a gun and I know where you live.' Ha! Ha! Ha! Only joking!)

As we kissed on the quiet hotel bed I noticed I'd given the slip somehow to that old male reserve in embracing. (She'd washed her mouth out, obviously.) I wasn't hanging on to a clear separateness of self. It was new to me to be shot of that. She smiled, and then, frowning like a tennis prodigy with her double-handed grip (O for a sophisticated man's sensibility), put raw and sore me inside her again without looking down. What a beautiful face (a calmness on it that I never saw at any other fucking time). I watched her ululating breasts as she watched mine. Her legs were folded right back, her knees to her shoulders, head to toes, like when she hits the crash mat and a testy hush falls over the commentary box.

The Grace of God lifted this sinner from the pornographic, from detached observation, from the commentary box. And it was that ancient dance where you neither of you know what's coming next. Thermal-currents of some marrow-hung fertility god call the shots: actions not your own. Occasionally his rude gargoyle face showed in one of ours.

She did a quick series of grabs and holds and then let go, her centre of gravity having shifted. I said 'hold me', her arms clasped round my back, and, as you've probably guessed by now Mr Rogers, I shot my fucking load. Still joined at the hip, we fell asleep.

Waking her that morning with my lips mouthing silent prayers on the kissing mouth of her cunt, and trying to stop myself coming as soon as we were socket-complete, and looking at her – eyes closed so tightly – I came again.

I love the term 'pearl necklace'. The image has the sense of pride with which a woman wears her lover's gift. The gift that's a token of her beauty, and his love for her, and which in the wearing makes her still more beautiful. Pearl necklace, though! Who are these jiz-artists, these cake-icers? I've never managed the necklace. Just sometimes the pearl hairnet, or the pearl glasses, ear-piece and bib set; sometimes a Stone

Roses picture sleeve, and sometimes the full-face visor. But not, alas, that morning.

Swooning, then awake together and her laying her leg over mine, in a friendly way.

. . . and me not wanting to disappoint, and if I only fuck her enough she'll love me again, and wanting to keep us here where we got on so well and everything was all right, the only place where it still was . . .

That morning I gave her a brooch of two small stones; and not pearls but rubies.

And I thought of the wedding toast in _The Deer Hunter_, when the bride spills two drops of red wine on her milk-white dress and it's a curse.

A curse had entered the hotel-room. It was the end of the line and there was nothing anyone could do. Not for all the milk in Lord Rayleigh's farm.

Four
BILLY HURLEY

If you happened to see Svetlana, I know she'd claim that us splitting up had nothing to do with me sleeping with Karen. She'd say it was just that I was getting to know the real her. 'You're not in love with me, you're in love with an idea of me,' she used to say. 'You don't know me.' Me and Svetlana had only just begun. I slept with Karen on New Year's Eve. I don't know, though – for all I see that I am the fantasist, the romantic, I wonder whether this tough old boot wanted something to believe in, and I broke it all up for her. But I don't know. I don't know anything. Leave me alone.

She was on holiday over New Year with her ex-boyfriend. She'd been jumping in Moscow and joined him in Prague. There were four of them together – her best friend and her beau, and so, she said, she couldn't cancel and leave all the others in the lurch. Plus, her ex- had organised it months before and we'd only met two weeks ago. I was much placated by a card that read: 'This may be your last Christmas without me, so make the most of it.'

On one of our late-night long-distance calls, she said, 'I don't want you to think of us as boyfriend and girlfriend.' I started getting upset. She told me I was getting the wrong end of the stick. But what was I to think? What else but that she was preparing me for a fall? I'd gone round, proud as a married-off prostitute, all shiny and new in the knowledge that now I belonged. And now this bolt from the blue. All she meant, she tried to tell me then, but now I know for myself, all she meant was something like, 'Let's find something out about each other first before locking in.' But I thought she was reclaiming sleeping-with-her-ex-boyfriend rights or something. She was annulling something, I thought. Either way, hope was wet ash in the mouth.

Assumptions learnt in the past blight the present. Smiling, I say to my American friend Jack, 'Oh, I thought you were lying before when you said you liked that track.' (I mix music, Ken. Nothing you'll have heard of, dear. And not remunerative enough to leave the language school where I teach.) And then, after I said that to Jack, I noticed – for about the only time in our friendship – a look of annoyance cross Jack's face. 'No! I wasn't!' he said in vehement New York tones, and I suddenly realised how rude this casual assumption of deceit was. The past blights the present. For two years I have felt as though my dustmen and milkman are on the verge of violent retaliation against me. I leave out too many bin-bags with the wrong sort of rubbish in them. I don't leave out any empty bottles for days, and then leave out three or four. A hiding is on its way. When Merry gave me a silver lighter the other day, I automatically assumed that she must have found it on the floor after a club night. The possibility that

51

she'd gone out and *bought* it for me didn't cross my mind, until she got narked that I hadn't thanked her for it. I assumed that Svetlana was treating me without respect, but it so happens that she didn't even let him *hug* her on holiday. (A stricture I would one day rue myself!)

Svetlana often looked vexed. She was worried about her next job. She was thirty-one. It was that veteran-footballer-seeks-pub moment. What to do next? She'd done a bit of commentary here and there, but chiefly she was writing a biography of her first husband's dad: Billy Hurley.

Corporal Billy Hurley, aged sixty-eight (retd.), had been one of the actual POWs in that camp *The Great Escape* was about. He'd never actually got out himself, though. He'd helped dig and been punished, helped dig and been punished much more. Fixed, resigned misery was etched in like Max Wall without the self-parody. You looked at his face and you thought he'd forgotten to put his false teeth in, but when he opened his mouth, there they were. His face looked like he'd lived in a place where gravity was twice the 14.7 pounds per square inch of the rest of the earth. His hanging, tugged face looked like he'd been living at two atmospheres of pressure.

Bald on top, dark hair back and sides. When a smile or half-laugh faded from his face, it looked like that gag where the artificialness of the smile is revealed in a moment of sudden and total collapse. You know, when you suddenly drop a smile to show a Walter Matthau/Bob Hope/Max Wall sourness beneath.

Every day was *not* a gift to this man. Incarceration

hadn't taught him to run over meadows every day he was free, FREE, *FREE!!* It had only taught him to see time as six-bar gates scratched into the wall with a broken spoon handle. It had taught him that a moment's excitement is followed by long and tedious misery, day-dreams by a cosh on the head. He learnt that someone is watching you at all times with a kind of bored ill-will, a lazy malice. The lesson was that he was an unlucky bastard, and always would be. That's how luck worked. He was also being denied fucking and drinking. When he got out, he vowed he'd do these all he could. His sense of catching up for lost time with women and drink usually meant that only his drink was still sitting next to him by the end of the evening in de-mobbed Leicester Square, or by the end of the seventies in Welwyn Garden City.

Billy Hurley's memory was blitzed by drink. A row of empty, clear-as-day Jack Daniels bottles stood on his kitchen sill.

Three or four dictaphone sessions in, it was clear that he couldn't remember anything about his own life at all.

Svetlana felt personally challenged by his defeatism. Born into communism, she hated what she saw as the American way whereby everyone she met had to recite their victimhood, their past. She observed that when someone comes up to you at a party, looks at their glass, and says, 'I'm really drunk', they are invariably about to say or do something which they are sober enough to know they shouldn't. In the same way, it seemed to her, when people recite their grievances, they are excusing behaviour or attitudes which they know are beneath them really.

The interviews with Billy Hurley were going nowhere, and so she began to make it up: a hat-trick he'd scored in a game against the German guards. She read this back to Billy, telling him that it was a transcript of their last interview mixed with a little independent research. She noticed he'd brightened up no end.

'Hey, that's great! I don't remember that. Ye-es. Heh heh. That sounds really good, really good.'

His mother appearing at the gates of the school one misty, sunny morning, with a packet of marbles which she passed through the fence, squeezing his little fingers twice. Were these fantasies of the upbringing Svetlana never had? I won't go into any of the grisly or spectacular recurrences of her childhood, but for this one quiet detail: she never had any toys. Well, one or two – but they weren't proper toys. These were the only toys Svetlana had: an antique tin soldier, a chess-set and a set of dominoes. She made a house out of the dominoes and put the chess-men in it.

Svetlana's parents came here from Romania when she was four. They'd thrown too many stones in too many demos to keep their posts in academe and television for long. Like so many middle-class liberal parents of the sixties and seventies, it seems, they insisted on still being children even if this meant making their children adults. Svetlana was an accident, to boot. The message was: 'If you're going to live in this house, you'd better do so as an adult.' Hence my oddly formal, ever-so grown-up, ultra-realist darling. (The lover is disgracefully ambivalent about the sufferings of the loved one. Would she be her otherwise? Until the first row, that is.)

When she read the scenes of a fantasy childhood back to Billy, his old man's eyes would water. Old blocks thawing. When the sobs came, his slack, raddled face was pulled about as if it were going through the G-force. 'Mom and pop, mom and pop.' The tears went all over his face as they found no way of going straight down so many leathery folds and creases, so much history.

She began to push the envelope. An affair with Vera Lynn. Its dark, sexual role play had Vera as dominatrix bitch commandant, Billy as tied-up Tommy Atkins; the lash, the escape, then the tables turned: 'Now, as you were saying, Mädchen, it is indeed an excellent rope for thrashing!' said Billy triumphant. Dame Vera – or just Vera as she was then, of course – jerked her head around frantically, her range of movement limited by gag and tether, as Billy's coarse builder's rope flailed down on her young naked haunches.

This was greatly to the surprise of the listening pensioner, who had always thought of himself as rather more inhibited than other men.

She gave him the next page to read as she was too embarrassed to read it out loud herself. He put on his Jim Callaghan reading-glasses. Under the large, thick lenses, his eyes looked enormous as if amazed by what he was reading.

Lash . . . _CRACK!_ Lash . . . _CRACK!_

'Mmnnnffggghff,' said Vera.

'We don't want to wake the Oberleutnant now, do we?' Lash . . . CRACK!

Vera's milk-white buttocks were soon striped with red, which shaded into purple an hour or so later, when Billy broke himself from her loving post-coital nuzzling embrace to make them both some Ovaltine and powdered egg.

'Hey, that's great! I don't remember that at all. Ye-es! Heh, heh. That sounds really good, really good. Goodness me!'

He started gardening and washing under his armpits. He started shaving in an enamel bowl over the kitchen sink, because that was where the sun came up in the morning. For twenty years he'd shaved in the shadow-cold sink upstairs. For twenty years each new day had announced itself as a chilly eclipse in the bathroom, as if some speechless gremlin of guilt made him feel that's all he deserved.

He started sight-seeing. He revisited the scenes of romantic haunts he'd never been to before. Running his hands over the flint of a ruined abbey where he'd lain one afternoon with Vera, a dreamy, reflective grin came to his lined face. He nodded to himself in sweet remembrance, while a shadow rolled swiftly across a field eager to meet the crazy man.

Every now and then he'd be standing in, say, a church that, when the sun went in, would be suddenly gutted of warmth and association. And he'd think, 'What am I doing here? An old man in the middle of nowhere with nothing in his head.' But this, he guessed, was normal. This was what it meant to be an old man visiting a past that doesn't exist anymore. And, hands in pockets, he sauntered back through the church porch into the daylight, humming, '*no, they can't take that away from me.*'

To Svetlana the new Billy Hurley was a complete vindication of her world-view. She thought that everyone was hanging on to past histories that they could let go of if they wanted to. (All right, then: *me*! *I* was hanging on to a past history which I could let go of if I wanted to!) 'I've never met anyone,' she'd say, 'whose childhood was as bad as mine, and yet I'm not miserable, so I don't see why anyone else should be.'

I was more persuaded by this than she knew. I was beginning to doubt the omnipotence of the past.

Still, in the days when I foolishly believed that arguments against women are ever won, I pressed on. 'The past conditions your expectations. You carry a memory just like metals do: the past stress, the present weakness.' (Svetlana heard in this a sick-note tone of excuses, I bet. Quite right, too. A suicide note's just a sick-note you write yourself.) 'A balance is struck between past and present. It's all in the balance. It's like a case I heard of a suicide,' I continued, digging my own grave. 'This guy took an overdose. They'd found him in the coma, and they'd managed to pump his stomach. He's sitting up in bed next morning – fresh pyjamas, primped pillows – saying, "I regret what I did. I'm grateful for this second chance, now that I finally realise just what a rare and precious gift life is." And the doctor's there saying, "That's as may be, but I don't think you'll survive the massive coronary you've got coming in about one hour."'

Forgetting he'd been banned from driving (Drink,

Austin Wolsey, the heatwave of '76, police horse, ditch), Billy bought a car and did some more sight-seeing.

He even attended a reunion bash at the Metropole in Brighton. He'd always passed on these things, bitterly. But now, well, it must be fate – look who was here: Vera! Out on the crowded dance floor, dancing with another man. Oh well, time moves on, he reflected magnanimously. He stared at her with proprietorial pride: yes, time had been good to her, his love. Her hair still blonde, not grey or silver, like anyone else her age. She was smiling at someone now, now, a smile he remembered so well. He stood staring at her for some time, smiling and nodding to himself. Vera. Vera. Vera.

He'd seen no one else he knew, or if he had they hadn't recognised each other. He'd stared at faces hoping that the slime of age would quicken to a young man's remembered mouth or grin – but no.

He was coming back from the buffet, loaded paper plate in hand, when suddenly he was right behind her. He would whisper their old secret language in her ear, a language he remembered so well, which would spark her back from the half-life of erotic compromise. And so, smiling – and the good Dame, ever-friendly having turned to meet this unknown veteran – he put his mouth to her ear, saying fondly, 'Hello you Kraut bitch. I'll be round the back, eh? Eh? You filthy German whore.' And, with a nod and a wink of his old etched face, he sauntered outside, hands in pockets, to wait for her.

Five
SOMEONE, SOMEWHERE, IN SOMERSTOWN _____

Karen got off the train that took her to London and, taking a number from her purse, phoned the solicitor's from a call-box outside Euston.

'Rosewood and Company,' said the voice inside the receiver.

'Hello, I was given your number by a friend. I need some advice.'

This woman at the other end sounded middle-aged. She stood inside one of the oldest and most respected legal firms in the land. At intervals in Karen's story she said, 'oh no ... are you all right?' Then she said, 'Are you in a call-box?'

'Yes.'

'Well give me the number and I'll call you right back.'

Karen hung up and stood in the quiet phone box. She scrunched two of her carrier bags back on the scratched metal shelf. The plastic bags then started crinkling outwards again in noisy slow-motion. Her feet tucked the bag on the floor further inside the booth. Here she was. Miles from home. A silent call-box in London. She glanced over her shoulder. She was in luck: no one was waiting. The phone rang.

Picking up the receiver, she had the sensation of being a seven year old playing telephones with another girl: the make-believe of 'you phone me up and I'll pretend to answer like I don't know who it is.'

'Hello?'

'Hello.' The lawyer extracted a few more details. This time in that tone of voice doctors use when they're all but certain of their prognosis, and are just mentally crossing off the last few double-checks. 'The first thing is that this is very clumsily done. I'm a defence lawyer. I work with criminals all the time – I know how they think. *Clumsy* people resort to violence much earlier than is needed. They don't understand that the best time to get at you is a few weeks before the trial. That's when most witnesses get done. Now, if he knew exactly what he was doing he'd have left it until the last few weeks so the police didn't get wind of it. So I think you're not in any immediate danger, and you have been – even though it doesn't feel like it – a bit lucky.'

A white van stopped outside at some traffic-lights, its passenger window level with the glass booth in which she stood. Leaning on a half-down window, an arm hanging out, a bored young man stared at her with impunity. The lights changed and the traffic pulled him off, still in the same position. She had looked up first when she felt him staring at her, and now she looked up a second time to confirm that he was gone.

'My advice to you,' the voice in the cracked black plastic receiver was saying, 'and this is off the record, obviously – is that you're doing the right thing. Don't testify. Make yourself scarce. Eventually the police will be on to other things. And after the case has been and gone and you haven't testified, this man won't have any axe to grind either.'

'Right.'

'But I do have to tell you that the law says you *could* get up to four years for not testifying.'

'What? Even though there's a contract out on me?'

'Regardless of the danger you're in. But my advice to you is – and this is off the record, as I say, between ourselves – to make yourself scarce.'

'Well, I was thinking of skipping the country.'

'That wouldn't be a bad idea.'

As is often the case with people giving advice that is hard, refined, top-grade, and given with concentration, the woman was impatient of interruption. She demanded higher attention than the merely conversational level from her listener. But now she had done, her tone was like it was at the beginning of the call: 'Any time you need to call me you can. Reverse the charge, whatever – just ask for me. Don't worry, there's no charge. Good luck. Bye. Good luck, Karen.'

And so began a year on hold. Karen felt as if someone had pressed a pause button on her life.

When she started to sign on in London the police, now wised-up to the fact that she was on the run, had her benefit stopped.

She got a job as a waitress in the West End and then in a small restaurant in Belsize Park.

The popular girl was a successful waitress. She did well on tips. She had the happy knack of knowing who she could be informal with. The other reason she did well on tips was the way she looked in black leggings with a white tea-towel double-folded and wrapped about her waist, like a microskirt that didn't quite cover her bottom. Her breasts were usually braless under a starchy white blouse, on which no male diner could not wish for something to spill and make transparent the rumour of brown – or was it pink? – nipple.

She had been sent to Coventry for two whole years at secondary school. Gary Christmas fancied her, but she didn't want to go out with him. Monica Jenkins was her friend but fancied Gary Christmas. Gary Christmas turned all the boys in her year against her, Monica Jenkins all the girls. Physically, Karen was untouched, because her sister Gina, even though a year younger, was pretty much the toughest girl in the lower school. But maybe this was a lesson in endurance which helped her now.

Home late from work in the still hours of two and three, when the siren calls are farther off on only the very worst estates, she sits on the floor and plays the better records of her hideout's collection with headphones on, so as not to wake her hosts, chain-smoking and pouring the last of the bottle of dry white wine she brought back from work into a lipsticked glass or mug.

For a spell she feels like she can't breathe, that she's muffled. She breathes in as far as she can, but still feels like all the air has just been trampled out of her lungs or that the oxygen isn't getting in. She has a hit off her Ventolin inhaler but she knows this breath-lessness isn't asthma.

When she starts crying, it is not out of sorrow, but out of a kind of stress.

Not to know they put the witness's address on statements as a matter of course, she suspects a bent policeman, working on the inside, tipped off Buzz for the attempted break-in. If this is so, then all the omniscient cables of information in the earth and sky are flexing against her: National Insurance number, bank sort code, passport number, London Electricity Board customer reference, phone number. 'I don't know if I'm just being paranoid,' she thinks; but wasn't that what she had said the day after the break-in – the day the contract was put out? She blamed herself. 'I shouldn't have got involved. Criminals only ever kill their own kind.' She even blamed herself for being in the pub that night – and this would've sounded as mad to her as you any other time.

About to cook herself some curry at 4 a.m., at the end of a not bad night in on her own with her flat-mate's record collection, she hears herself saying, 'Why not? Why not?' in an impish way. She stops in the middle of the kitchen, the saucepan in her hand stayed in mid-air. 'Where did that phrase come from?' she asks herself. Now she has it. That was what Father Dunphy used to say with a mischievous smile, when enthusing over someone's vague suggestion that they climb Snowdon a second time that trip, or open another big polythene bag of pre-prepared sarnies. 'Why not? Why not?' he'd say as if there was some-thing naughty in these things. Now that she blames herself, everything in life seems profoundly connected, like the plot of a film or a novel. She thinks of all the little ways in which she's wandered away from that safe world in which she'd buried sandwich crusts under rocks, and thrown apple cores at the boys. She has left the path of righteousness which she'd enjoyed without knowing it. An egotism here, an infidelity there.

Her appearance has become juvenile. Her dyed blonde hair – now longer – is in pig-tails. She now wears mini-skirts with pop socks.

INT. NIGHT. *NELLIE.*

KAREN: I felt sometimes like I was the one that was in prison; I felt like I'd served a two-year prison sentence for something I wasn't guilty of. I couldn't go and visit my friends; I was forced to leave Wythenshawe, which was my home; I had no possessions – three carrier bags and that was it, feeling constantly on edge . . . it was *horrible* . . .

She never knew when the police were going to catch up with her either, and so, bizarrely, she felt like someone who was both serving a prison sentence and yet somehow also on the run. It didn't escape her mind that that had been Buzz's exact situation on the night of the murder.

In another way, it wasn't like being in prison at all. Unlike a lag, there was no one else, *no one* who knew what it was like. Who could know what this was like?

Someone else was dictating her life. Every stubbed toe, every disconnected phone or electric, and all the tedium of reconnection, each lonely night short of cash – all were forced by another hand. She felt like someone or something was watching her at all times with a lazy but vicious malice. But then you couldn't look at it like that; if you did you'd be eaten by bitterness. There wasn't an ounce of self-pity in her. 'I won't let him ruin my life,' she said. But the next thing to go was the love of her life.

Mark had been in the Rose Cottage with her that night. (Remember the student vet punching the wounds together? That was him.) Back in London she was all alone. Mark lived in Stoke, and he wasn't on the phone. She had nobody there. Cut off from her family and friends, he was the only contact she had, and so he always bore the brunt of it all when she went to visit him. She thought to herself that she was debilitating him: 'He's got his shit to be getting on with, too, I suppose.'

They were lying naked in his single bed, curled up together, her behind him with her arms around him, and her legs folded into the Z-shape of his. It had been a good night they had spent together but she'd been worried that it was the type of night they might have had before her nightmare began. On one level this was excellent – if she could be happy she would be, and she loved their revels – but on another level, she needed him to act like he knew what she was going through.

She lay against his back, staring at the wall. In a poster blu-tacked to the wall a fat and grunge-bearded, thirty-five-year-old rocker in an American desert was a picture of aggressive self-absorption. Mark, slim and grunge-bearded, turned out the side-light. They were both silent and settled down for sleep, when Karen quietly said, 'I need help.'

'Don't be silly,' came the voice, its mouth distorted by the pillow. 'No you don't. You're coping really well. You're really strong. You don't need anyone.' He had told himself that it was good medicine for her if he made out that it was no big thing, really.

She knew at this moment that he couldn't help her because he didn't understand. She knew it clearly. She went ahead with the night-long row for the hell of it, but she knew then that it was over.

Like any man close to sleep, Mark was slow to realise he was in a row. (Wishful thinking always makes us imagine we might be able to go back to our lovely kip any second! Folly! Folly!) Slow to realise the seriousness of the row, he never made up the distance lost by his slow start. At the point when he should have been turning on the light to put his arms round her, he was only just rolling on to his back to listen to what she was saying. Then, at the point when he should have been looking her in the eyes with an expression that said 'What are your demands?', he was only then turning on the light and trying to put his arms around the woman who had just got up from the bed. At the point when he should have been getting out of bed and making a cup of tea before sitting down with her at the kitchen table to thrash out a stratagem, he was trying to catch her eye to show her his 'What are your demands?' look. And at that point, when he'd finally given up all idea of sleep, when finally he had resigned himself to a night of argument, of sacrifice, and yes, of being the man she could lean on . . . Karen was back in bed, settling down to sleep. He was left, flapping in the wind, saying, 'Let's talk about this; we need to talk about this! Come on, Karen, we need to talk about this! Don't just go to sleep!'

The next evening Mark and Karen found themselves on the sofa watching a wildlife documentary about birds in Iceland. They were shoulder to shoulder, and that, thought Mark, was something at least. (Earlier, they'd gone for lunch at the cafe in the park. In the self-service queue, Mark had put his arm tentatively round Karen, and they had held hands, briefly, in the park. Karen had soon disengaged her hand though.) Part of the Icelandic birds' courting ritual is that the male bird lays a twig across the female's feet. Karen thought this the sweetest thing she'd ever seen, and went into peals of affectionate laughter. The female would sometimes peck the twig off, and the male would humbly replace it. Something in the male's timid offer of perpetual shelter delighted her, something in the way it was both gracious and yet dumbly demonstrative too.

She came out of the bathroom at bedtime, wearing just a long T-shirt. Mark told her to close her eyes and stand in the middle of the sitting-room.

'What are you going to do?' she asked, seeing him approaching on all-fours.

'Close your eyes!'

She felt his hair sweep by her shins.

'OK,' he said, having backed off.

She opened her eyes, and couldn't see anything at first. She looked down and saw the twig lying across both her feet. 'Ah! That's so sweet!' she laughed. He clasped his arms round her pale bare legs. She bent over and put her palms on his back. He climbed up and they kissed.

Next morning she got out of bed first to make some tea. While the water was heating in a saucepan on the ring, she went into the sitting room. She found the twig lying on the table with the debris of the night before. She picked it up. No, Mark's romantic gesture was empty really: he wasn't going to help her. She put the twig up on the bookshelf as something he could keep and remember her by.

She went to stay in Archway with Kevin, her boy-friend before Mark. At first Kevin was like Albert Schweitzer. 'Penis? Oh I think I've got one here somewhere . . . [pats pockets] . . . now, where did I see it last? . . . [looks around floor] . . .' They were both so touched and heartened with themselves for being able to relate to each other non-sexually in a time of crisis, that they started shagging.

As soon as Kevin had met The Extraordinary Svetlana, however, Karen couldn't stay there anymore. She left the next day, not to return until that fateful New Year's Eve when Kevin fucked up. She stayed with Victoria (a friend from Hulme now in London), Elizabeth (a New Zealander), François (a gay Austrian), and Anna (a Venezuelan) – and also at mine for a week or so – three plastic bags under this very desk I'm writing on now.

I was more scared than her. Returning to my front door at night, what assailants lay hidden in the alley by the bins, or crouching in the hall? Waiting and listening, before they tortured me for hcr whereabouts, and then just tortured me anyhow because they were such hardened gangsters that they had to do the unspeakable to get the merest flicker of enjoyment in carnage-visor eyes. And so, descending the dark basement stairs, I'd pretend not to be alone: 'All right, Kevin, Dean, Gary, Jeggsy. Blimey, put that shooter away! How's the Kung Fu going, Tony? Cor guvnor, bleedin' hell, strike a light, Chris, Steve! Lads!'

One day early in her exile she phoned her dad. Joey Doonan was a short, barrel-chested, muscular builder, with curly grey woollen hair, and a forehead with twice too much skin on it. The brow of a larger man, its fleshy folds rippled thickly, giving him the air of a giant puzzling over which leprechaun had stolen his body and swapped it with his. A builder by trade, he was very much one of 'the boys'. If any vengeful, Irish posse were got up to sort someone out, his name

would be on the call-up roster. If you wanted someone beaten up by one man alone, Joey would be your
man, even now in his middle-age. Never for money,
mind, but for a favour given or returned, or even im-
partially for rectitude's sake. Joey was your man. If
you were Irish, you might go into one of the drinking
clubs and say, 'I'm looking for Joey.'

'Which Joey?' asks the landlord.

'He has a frown of perplexity.'

'Does it give him the air of a giant puzzling over
which leprechaun has stolen his body and swapped it
with his?'

'Yes.'

'Oh, Joey *Doonan*.'

It was odd that from this stumpy bull had come
thin, waify, often ailing Karen. 'Very fucking odd,'
thought Joey ruefully, looking through his wife's
photo-album of the sixties, at men he didn't know the
name of and would never ask. Contrary to Joey's
twenty-seven-year-old grudge, however, they *were*
father and daughter. More than that, she was, as they
say, her father's daughter. She was more like him in
character than the stocky Gina, who more resembled
him. The quality father and daughter had most in
common (apart from being short) was toughness. But
who could have seen it in the girl? Her limp-wristed
hand gestures were florid and almost camp; she was
better spoken than her sister until drunk. (The Doo-
nans had moved to Wythenshawe from Leeds when
Karen was twelve: Gina still sounded broad Leeds;
the parents still sounded Irish; but Karen sounded
like she'd grown up in a smart suburb of Leeds and

had only been bussed into the Doonan household for breakfast and important rows.)

She was at her most fey and Oscar Wildey/Scott Fitzgeraldey when talking about her Mick progenitor. Talking *about* him, that is, but not when talking *to* him. Then she spoke with her native Leeds accent again.

'I just want you to know that I've been in this trouble . . .' She went on to give her father the merest outline of the tale over the phone. She glossed over things and tried to ignore his breathing, which was growing heavier and heavier throughout, until it caught on his vocal chords and he spoke.

'Who is it?'

'It doesn't matter.'

'Is he black?'

'Look, Dad. I don't think that's really relevant.'

'He's black isn't he?'

'Yes he is, but the reason I'm phoning was just – '

'Well, what's he called then?'

'Look, don't think you can sort it out, because you *can't*.'

Joey went quiet. He could hear that Karen was trying to tell him something without telling him something. He could hear that it was something important, but the penny had yet to drop. Karen pictured the fleshy furrows of his perplexed brow, his deep-set eyes staring straight ahead as if he were about to headbutt Thought itself.

'I *know* people. These people have got to be shown; they don't understand – '

'No, Dad, no. You'll just get me into worse trouble.'

He went silent again. He tried to attune himself to the penny he could feel about to drop. It seemed nearer now. 'I can have guns out today!'

'No Dad,' she said sternly. And then, emphasising each syllable as if it were Morse Code, she added, '*there's nothing you can do.*'

The longest pause and then the penny dropped. With the regret of a strongman who knows his strength is useless, he asked, 'Do they know where Gina lives?'

'Yes dad.'

Six
THE DAY BEFORE GLEN WAS MURDERED _____

Orlando is working on his eyes. He wants a stone-eyed stare. He wants *kill-a-motherfucker-like-it-ain't-nothing* eyes. Hard eyes. Dead eyes.

He has a fantasy. It takes place on the metro down in London. Or Miami. Somewhere he's not known. He's wearing shades. All you can see is his baby face. Some local gangstas are fucking with everyone on the carriage. He's contentedly listening to his Discman. They whisk his Loco shades off him. He slowly turns his slow gaze up at them. They see the eyes. They fumble apologies. They know they are *way* out of their depth, and that if they're really lucky it *may* end here. They hand the Locos back, folding them first and you can hear each arm click against the frame. They leave the tube.

Or, say, his stone eyes staring out from the photo at the top left of his arrest sheet. The police are taken aback by the *lack* in his eyes. A deadness. Eyes that would never show emotion. Cold, dull eyes. A catatonic's eyes but without the lethargy.

Every time he deals, every time he threatens, every time they drive at a contemptuous fifteen miles per hour through enemy territory, every time he sees something which later makes him cry – like when Buzz stabbed Troy – it's all part of the eye-hardening process.

Shirley wants something else from his eyes. 'Your eyes – they're too cold,' she says to him. 'I don't like it when your eyes are so flinty.' This troubles him. She won't let him near her when his eyes are stone. 'Contain yourself,' she says, pushing him away, when he has the blind eyes of a statue of lust.

'I don't trust Buzz, Shirley,' he says, getting up from the mattress and putting his Filas on.

'Tell him. He'll respect that.'

"Ash? Rock? Grass?' Orlando is working the midnight to dawn shift. Standing on the frontline outside the poolie, waiting for executives in Audis or scally-packed Vauxhall rattlers, or raveheads in Golfs and Pandas, or passers-by, students and locals on foot. "Ash? Rock? Grass?' Standing in the cold. A police van parks up and kills its lights. Through the open sliding door, its handbrake ratchet can be heard in the still night. They'll be there for half an hour or so. Ninety-five per cent chance the van is empty, but it might just be a raid. But after only five minutes the scuffers turn their van headlights on again and pull away.

No one. Nothing.

A car comes by, morale as high as the fuel-gauge. How do they get *their* fucken money? He knows their score and disappears into the poolie, comes out again and leans into their front window. Boy girl, girl boy, black white, black brown. All the while chatting, money and wraps change hands. They drive off and he hears the bass beat bumping.

No one. Nothing.

"Ash! Rock! Grass!"

Some nights the only other person at three or four a.m., just down the street, would be this lone five-foot-four white Christian. He'd stand there in his moustache, tartan shirt and Christ-style anorak, holding a Bible. Some of the frontline thought this man was a narc. Orlando knows he isn't. Orlando thinks in pictures, not words: in complex patterns, twisting coloured structures, Imagist flashes. He sees the peculiarly dull clothes of the Christian evangelist. They all dress like that. As if really they're transcendent beings who have merely assumed the guise of ordinary late twentieth century folk as gleaned from encyclopaedias. They dress like the drawings of *representational* man in *Watchtower*.

Occasionally, on a slow night, two or three homiez would go up and talk to this man, smiling like dolphins nosing and nuzzling round a human who has clumsily joined them at fifty fathoms; inquisitive and profoundly detached as they observed this smaller being who lived on 'terra firma' but chose to come down here!

As it is just the two of them tonight, Orlando nods curtly to the Christian – the general to the civilian.

Buzz and Orlando are in a large room above a shop. It's a bogus shop: a year ago, to massage the hopeless jobless statistics, the government gave starter funds to new businesses. The landlady put two market-stall blouses and a skirt in the window and collected £500. Above the fictional shop which is really a flat is the fictional flat which is really a shop. Here Buzz sits in front of some scales. Big grocer's scales with stainless-steel scoops. He's working with sunglasses on as if blinded by all the bright white stuff in polythene sachets. He wears a blue bandana on his head. He boshes up with a swift, even fluency, grinning to himself. Even though it's nippy out, the sun has made a greenhouse of the flat. The windows are thick with condensation. Buzz salivates noisily as he measures the last of the powder out. Orlando keeps thinking Buzz is sucking his teeth at him over something he's done wrong. Globules of sweat rest just below Buzz's bandana as big as raindrops on a humid day.

'I don't trust you.'

Buzz doesn't look up. 'I know.'

'You're like a machine, Buzz.' Buzz continues looking down and bagging up. Orlando feels trepidation. What will Buzz's reaction be? Has he pushed it too far?

Buzz cackles and looks at Orlando. 'I'm machine man!'

'The machine man,' grins Orlando, relieved.

'*Now you know why they call raggamuffin Rambo. Ayeayeayeay!*' Orlando's walking along, singing to himself. The way he sings it has none of the strident nasality of the reggae toaster's sharp, jokey original. In his mouth it sounds like an after-hours Matt Monroe crooning in a shoo-be-doo cocktail lounge. When he gets off Souvrayney Street he'll stop humming. Farewell to the stress-free and familiar. The smell of ginger spice, pepper and paprika from the shop owned by that Scottish Asian with his tartan hat and pre-emptive aggression.

'*What's in the bag, Orlando?*' If the cops stop him he reckons that'll probably be the first question. It's a designer black vinyl bag like a paperboy's. Expensive, too. What will he say? 'Homework'? 'College books' and give a sly, coy, clean-kid smile while thinking all the time down which alley to give it toes? He could slam the bag on the broken glass crowning that wall, and belly over. He's unlikely to be stopped: it's an irregular, unusual errand. Imagine, he thinks, one gang trading with another, the Reds on Hogdale and Arkness.

The Reds had done their half of the bargain. They'd sent over several kotchels of E to the Arkness Estate, and taken pride in how good it was (all doves).

There's a crack-drought over on Hogdale. Their coke comes from Peru. In the late eighties, it came in through what was left of the industrial shipping coming into northern docks, sometimes in, say, a foreign lorry's petrol tank: below the level of the petrol, there'd be another tank welded on to the internal wall.

By the early nineties most of what came in was through 'mules': some forlorn Mexican cleaning-woman with 28 plastic sachets swallowed into her gut, the promise of a visa, and a glowing description of the developed world's stomach-pumps.

And then they sussed that too.

Supply squeezed, demand booming (pre-Cantona and nothing to live for) – it called for radical solutions. And the most radical of all was the one the Reds over on Hogdale bought into. A plan to use migratory swallows from Peru as flying mules.

Swallows return to the same nest year after year. Every spring the Peruvian swallow nests near reed-beds in the North West. Their man in Lima was massaging two-and-a-half gram deals down the swallows' dark gullets á la pâté-de-fois-gras, the swallow's beak silently opening and closing in fear and broken protest.

A bearded, middle-aged hippy who once ran a rural amphetamine factory with his cottage-farm wife, converted their cavernous, musty, dank, tumbledown barn into swallow heaven. The immense barn was stocked with grubs and lice and was soon rammed with swallows, upwards of four hundred. It was like a swallow rave with all the tweety din and their strobey movements. Thus, by October, just before they flew back to the Andes, the swallows left with fond memories of the grub-teeming barn. *'Y'all come back soon now, y'hear?'*

If they didn't all come back to the actual barn, the plan was to take guns down to the reed-beds – and to the ones at Overdowns near Southport – and shoot them down. (At last, that Kangol fantasy come true! Remember all those inner-city deerstalkers and Pringle hunting-style corduroy a decade or so ago? Now they would be the thing itself. Only not with two-bore and shot, but Smith & Wesson and semi-automatic. Here they go a-gathering swallows – plus unlucky shrikes, godwits and jack snipes.)

A lot of money was sunk into this and not just by the Hogdale estate. The Yardies sent up one of their men who was based in Bristol. He was there to count how many birds they got. Otherwise, it was reasoned, the English end would be able to take a fine harvest and then say, 'Sorry there's just £2,000 in the E-mail, but only a dozen birds showed up.' There was even a Peruvian counting man flown over; and this yardie up from St Paul's was to be the Peruvian's in-the-field support.

The first flock in was only about four-and-twenty birds, but they were all holding. There were cheers – it was like the successful-return scene in *633 Squadron* or *The Dam Busters* – cheers and jubilation.

Cold hands devised new ways of filleting which wouldn't split the polythene. (In through the Gary Glitter with the blade, and then kind of pulling upwards and outwards as you drew the knife-edge over the belly towards the neck.) When the stench got bad everyone upped their scarves, or put their noses in the tops of their coats. At the start, everyone was using regular Friday night knives. Then someone brought in a butcher's gutting tool (blood-soaked string wound tight around the handle). They waited for the next flock to fill the sky.

Under hot navigational sun, each day was warmer than the last, and the polythene sachets began to melt. They became semi-permeable membranes through which cocaine and heroin osmoscd, giving the swallows a slow-release hit somewhere over the equator. (The drugs were of a non-European quality which on the street would have cost each swallow upwards of £500.)

—————————————————

The formation 'V'-sign degenerated into feather-ruffling mid-Atlantic somersaults and tumbles. Some just folded and fell. When the last of the few who did make it to Overdowns flew in, they overshot it and went right on through to that beach in Southport where by night Scousers razz stolen cars, and Dalglish walks his dog by day. These few swallows cawed down the beach, oblivious to being outnumbered by ten thousand sandpipers. Like sandpipers the swallow-mules had decided to follow the edge of waves up and down the sandy beach, as well. The sandpipers and peewits stopped to stare inquisitively at the swallows queering their pitch. They hopped and fluttered out of the way a little, to let them through. The swallows were walking along with their beaks open and their wings out as if flying.

Most of the swallows simply chose a different course. As the hard pure drugs coursed through their tiny systems high in the sky, the birds started going off the usual route. Many of them showed up at Stonehenge, or perched on the Orb's stack at Glastonbury. Some swallows made it to the Milk Bar in Amsterdam.

In Manchester swallows flocked hopefully behind Shaun Ryder's BMW. Shaun Ryder wrenched his neck, throwing frantic looks through the rear-window. He accelerated, looking back through the straight black lines of the heated rear window. The birds were still there. He picked up his mobile, and punched in his dealer's number.

'Yeah'.

'Clyde, Shaun –'

'What's up?'

'You've sold me fookin' acid 'ere!'

In the Cheshire village of Glossop the butcher put a sign in the window saying 'SORRY. SWALLOW PIE SOLD OUT'; while a consortium of farmers from that same village (farmers who were on exceedingly good terms with the butcher), placed an ad in the music papers offering their land should any rave convoys be passing that summer.

Ornithologists noticed a birdsong new to the Peruvian swallow. At first it sounded like the cry of the roseate tern (*sterna dougalli*). A drawn-out 'aach-aach' with a softer 'tchu-ick.' After repeated plays on baffled tape-recorders, however, birdlovers were forced to concede that the two bpm 'aaach-aaach's followed the bass sequence of 'I Like To Move It' by Reel 2 Real (featuring The Mad Stuntman).

Nests were discovered in Norfolk in unusual pyramidal or wig-wam shapes. In an arable field six or seven swallows were seen clustering round a scarecrow, whose head was a scuffed and punctured plastic football. They appeared, said an observer, to be trying to make friends.

_____

By now Orlando is on the Hogdale Estate itself. This is Hogtown. By a row of garages, a fat white man demonstrates a home-made rifle made out of steel piping to a thin white man. Orlando passes through climbing frame and swings. His tread is surprised by the spongey, springy, bouncy black asphalt of the playground. He's to go up to the third floor of the council block. He doesn't want to look like he's lost.

It's not fair. He had wanted to show them his unimpeachable cool. His clear, untroubled eyes. But he is troubled. Not because he's walking into the heart of enemy territory. He's nervous because of the weight of doubt Buzz has dropped into the black bag. Orlando knows that Buzz is after Glen, because Glen is going around saying that Buzz had jumped on the drugs he sold him. Buzz says he's going to do Glen in the Rose Cottage. But now – is Orlando taking jumped-on drugs to the Hogdale estate?

Orlando doesn't know enough about the product to test it with a dab of finger on expert tongue, he doesn't have his own computer-scales.

A turn in the concrete staircase. He stops in the pissy shade, leans back against the soft bag against the hard wall, breathes deeply, tucking his nose into the neck of his Fila shirt so as not to be inhaling enemy urine.

When he gets to Floor 3, staircase F, a watchman leaning on the balcony stares as he walks by. Hard to tell what that look is saying. Is it, 'can't *believe* you're here, because you being here is really taking the piss.

Man, I won't even bother starting in on you myself because they will kill you indoors when they see where you from.' Or is it recognition? Does his immobile stare – oh, he's got the eyes, most definitely the eyes – mean that he knows and acknowledges and even respects Orlando's business? Balcony Watchman is a couple of inches shorter than six-foot slim shaved-head Orlando, but twice as wide. Corn-rowed hair, puggy, light-tan face with thin Chinese eyes.

The door's open. Orlando walks into the flat. Deep, tangly, tawny, shaggy carpet. The same posters he's seen in other flats (Smith & Wesson .38, side-on; that charcoal drawing of the sulky-but-cute Rasta tot), only here framed and mounted. It is just someone's flat that they've taken over for this transaction.

Suddenly to take the deal out of the bag seems a bit minor league. He hands over his brand-new, black vinyl bag as well. Has he left anything embarrassingly personal and detailed in there? Anything with his home address deep down in the lining of the bag?

It's Massif he gives the heavy bag over to, whom he knows 'from time'. Massif wears a black Fred Perry and jeans, and seems second in command, Orlando notices with surprise, to a pure Affo. This man has a smiling Yoruba face. He wears those 'ripped' jeans that you buy with brown leather already sewn under each 'tear' in the denim: a style for those less confident than white grunge-children that the world will see that this is fashion not poverty. He wears the slip-on shoes of the African continent (alligator-scaled), with white socks.

Orlando, and every black or red he knows, skits

Africa-man: 'Ma fadda has boort a new hut,' they go, mimicking the old-Empire Nigerian accent. Their un-hip-ness, their meaningless wealth, meaningless because they don't know to spend it on what anyone else would spend it on. Often mad, Africa man, thinks Orlando. They'd been fourteen of them had tried to get Louis Fantayne's brother on the ground one night, when pipe-head Louis was giving it the big 'un. But this African had swung with a car bumper and they'd given up. They *could not* get him on the ground. Orlando feels the Africans kind of shouldn't be so good at fighting, what with their degrees and pilot's licences and dentistry qualifications.

This man doesn't seem mad at all. He's sharp. He's calm. His green-and-white striped shirt still has the folds in it from the shirt-box. He has the eyes, too (Grade A), bloodshot and heavy. His Nigerian clothes, well they just seem like clothes . . . Massif passes him the paperboy bag, he doesn't even look at it. He just puts it in the corner down by the side of his armchair. Impressive. That's saying: 'I know you wouldn't *dare* fuck with us; however, if you have chosen to take that stupid, mad option, we shall soon find you.' The African smiles gently and half-looks at Orlando for half a second.

Should he stay? Does anything need to be said? Orlando nods toward a couple of faces he knows from around, and from those other, lost planets of school and college. A couple of the eight or so men in there have already gone back to watching the video. (It's not out on video yet. It's not in the cinema yet. Judging from the ropey quality, someone must have been standing on the film lot over the director's shoulder with a palmcorder.) And Orlando knows he has already been committed to memory by all of them.

'Mission complete, that's when me feel irie, on me body there's no fat, it is strickly lean, now you know why they call Raggamuffin Rambo.' (Shoo-bee-doo-bee-doo!) Walking back from Massif's, his pulse settles as he regains the Methodist Centre: his own area. He returns to a familiar thought. There are, it seems to him, only two ways of looking at the world. As he walks along he does the two movements of the eyes which go with the only two ways there are of looking at the world. One way is harder, narrower, and the other is softer, wider. Shallowly or deeply. Kindly or meanly. Looking at a thing for what you could get from it, or looking at the thing itself. All life was this civil war between the two ways of looking at the world.

He sees a young mum bend over a pram, and puts the look in his eyes that Buzz has. He finds himself bunching his eyes up. Looking at the world in this way, he checks out her bending-over arse, the knicker outline, the cheapness of the jeans, the ripped polythene of the pram – see – the fatness of the baby, the drying drool on its chin.

Then he looks at the scene the other way. His round, young brown eyes see a mixture which is something like the mum's patience, her quiet enjoyment of the baby (pausing a few moments to talk to the chubby picknee as she puts the box of man-size tissues which have fallen on the pavement back into the buggy's under-tray), how she doesn't go 'paranoid-whitey' now, when she notices him staring. Having adjusted the shopping bags hung over the buggy's handles, she moves on. He checks out the arse too (oh well). The panty line is gone now she's up straight. How well she's kept her figure since the nightclub days when she landed her husband of the mansize tissues.

Damn! Buzz and the other faces don't go into these daydreams. Can't afford to, thinks Orlando. He needs to be always thinking what's the next move, who's thinking what, where the next possible danger might come from. Suddenly alert, Orlando jerks a look across the street. An old man in a brown suit and mini-trilby backs out of a shop, pretending to listen to what the garrulous Italian shopkeeper within is saying. The old man says, 'OK then, OK then.' There is a polite little chuckle in his voice, hoping each 'OK then' will be the last. Finally he gets his 'Cheerio then' in. Orlando jerks his head back. Where was he? Yeah – Buzz and the others are always thinking what's the next move, who's thinking what, where the next possible danger might come from. Who's got designs on you? On your pitch? Who is vulnerable? He looks back the twenty yards or so at the mum for any dangling half-open handbag. Rich men, he reasons, are always looking *all* the time, always had an eye for the main chance.

Here there used to be a whole block. Now there's just an open field of spent bonfires, stony rubble and weeds (the green shoots of recovery). Lone sounds come and go. A car bang-bangs over a pothole, plunging muddy water from deep down. Sometimes it seems like his energy and the babble in his head is all that's between him and the dead weight of slackness all around.

A stray dog scuttles past, looking at Orlando insolently, its long claws noisily scraping the pavement four times a second.

A short cut. He lifts a buckled panel of corrugated iron from the window of a gutted, smoke-blackened, red-brick terrace. If he squeezes through he'll get his clothes all fouled up. Twists of burnt bacofoil in a corner unaccustomed to the light. He lets the corrugated-iron swing back, and is surprised by how much noise it makes. And then the immense silence flows back again.

Back on the main drag. A JCB has freshly ploughed up new earth where, an indecently short time ago, the entire Turner Estate had been. All that's left now is the rusted shell of the playground: every swing ripped clean away, leaving not even the chains; the see-saw burnt. It looks like a hurricane has whipped through that playground, or kids with a demonic amount of steam to let off.

He crosses a cobbled street with decayed Georgian houses, passes the modern terraces of Hogarth Close, and then, not just a house, not just a street, but an entire estate boarded up.

Orlando remembers the very polite, respectable old Polish couple who for years were the last inhabitants of the block of flats across the street, now boarded-up. They lived on the corner of the second floor. Everybody else had moved out. Half the derelict windows were smashed. The council even came and boarded up a few. He remembers the lino corridor where, aged about twelve, he and his friends used to ride bikes and light fires. Once, smoking a draw or playing football in the passageway, they heard a piano playing classical music. He remembers the window-boxes that the old Poles or Czechs (or whatever they were) put out. Even the flowers, it seemed, were more aware of what was going on than that quiet couple. 'Oh shit,' the flowers thought, when they saw where they were, trying to keep their heads down as much as possible and not look too flowery.

He goes over to Buzz's to report back the delivery. This he does by the merest of nods, which is returned by an even more understated nod.

All the faces are there. All round at Buzz's to sample the new batch. (Columbian, ships.) Not as crack, but as cocaine. These are masters not servants, after all. Top boys.

Orlando asks himself if he should refuse. That would show he was to be trusted, his strength of character. Or should he partake in this sacrament of the fact that he is now a player? Slurpee offers him a line. He nods quickly. As he straightens up, Slurpee puts his hand on Orlando's shoulder, and looks him in the eye, saying, 'I used to be anti-taking drugs myself, but I find that my attitude towards drugs is changing now that I've got some cash.'

Orlando stares at the rolled-up twenty, unfurling in his palm in slow jerky stop-starts like a time-delay film of pupae unhatching. After a time he tunes into what Slurpee is saying to the room.

'You know Churchill used to take these cocaine lozenges. During the war his doctor was prescribing them for him. And 'cos he got them from his doctor, they would have been really pure as well.'

'Crack-sweets.'

'And he used to only need two hours sleep at night, and he'd be dancing every night, throwing out all these jokes, then three hours sitting up in bed surrounded by the war cabinet, while he drew up plans on a tea tray which would win the war. And when you think about it, all those speeches of his sound like a guy who's just done a line of toot: "We shall fight them in the air, we shall fight them on land, we shall fight them on the beaches, and then we're gonna rake the beaches and make them really smooth, pick all the pebbles out, and then we're gonna arrange our CDs alphabetically A to Z!"'

Orlando feels grateful to Slurpee. Yeah, Buzz likes to lick a rock or do a line, thinks Orlando, and he's a businessman. He doesn't fuck up, he can't afford to. Businessmen do it. Top businessmen. Now and then.

He pushes his fizzy-itch nose with the palm of his hand. Where has he seen that gesture? He smooths the note flat, thoughtfully. Buzz. Buzz does that *all the time*. Oh yeah, that's it. He holds the twenty pound note up to the light. In the white watermark in the purple twenty, he notices for the first time a familiar face. But the revealed face, noticed in the white cloud for the first time, is much sterner here than he's ever seen her before.

What did he have me take over in the bag?

Orlando looks up at Buzz. Buzz's sunglasses are on his forehead now, head tilted back to balance them there. The vapour trail of a smile is still on his face, but he isn't listening to Slurpee anymore. He is looking at Orlando. Orlando can see that Buzz is trying to see what he is thinking.

Seven
STATIONS OF THE GUN ⎯⎯

It's illegal to own a gun; but they don't say you can't
own a bit of a gun. In British cities the practice is to
break the gun down and distribute it here and there
for safe-keeping. The muzzle with your mum, the clip
with your nan, the ammo with your uncle or whatever.
There is a quirky, eccentric British by-product of this.
Before killing someone you have to do a tour of your
relatives, spending long hours sitting, tea and Lincoln
biscuit in hand, listening to the old folks. The Angel
of Objective Truth holds the records of how many
murders were prevented by the benign tedium of
avuncular chats cooling the blood.

It was a Berretta .98F from the Falklands. Manu-
factured as a semi-automatic, but by the time Orlando
bought it, the firing pin had been filed down so that it
was fully automatic. You could spray six bullets with
one squeeze if you really wanted to.

The stock and firing-mechanism were at his
mum's, up in the small inspection loft over his old
bedroom. He'd been worried about some robber
crawling from the loft of another flat on the same floor
and stealing it, or one of his mum's Mr Fixit boyfriends getting busy up there, so he'd hidden the parts

in his old hamster cage, in a nest of chopped-up paper. He pocketed the gun parts in the knee of his big red and black trousers, baggy like on Riker's Island where belts are not allowed.

When he came downstairs into the kitchen, his mum was sitting on one of those stools which fold out as a step-ladder.

Two weeks ago, she had bought him a grey American college sweatshirt. The logo read 'ORLANDO HIGH'. She didn't understand why he wouldn't wear it. Orlando had left it there twice already. It now lay folded neatly on the kitchen fitment next to her and her good smell of hairspray and smoke. Coolly, she watched him size up the scene and stop in the middle of the room.

'You wear sports gear all of yous,' she began. 'I don't see why you won't wear this.' Orlando gave her an aw-come-on-let-me-off giggle, but she wasn't to be put off. '*Raiders, Shaq, Fila,*' she went on, pointing at his vest. She was cross. Like all young mums she hoped for some of the dividends of being a big sister as well. She thought of herself as still in touch. She had hoped he'd appreciate the pun in 'HIGH', and that his friends would, and that she would get her props as a cool mum.

She had been quite beautiful when younger. Nowadays, she'd look young one day, and the next she'd look old. Her hair was 'relaxed' by style, brittle by texture, shoulder-length and black. Sitting smoking on the kitchen stool with the steps folded under it she stared at him impassively. Her beige cheeks hollowed on her long Dunhill an instant, as she sat cross-legged, now resting the elbow of her cigarette arm on the other hand which was across her breasts. Her stare became impatient. Orlando beamed like a loon and didn't say anything. She said: 'I mean, Clifford wears these. He's got a Yale top I seen him in and – '

She stopped too late. She knew she'd lost the argument right there, and he gave her a sardonic Bill-Cosby-over-half-moon-glasses look: 'my point exactly.'

She got down from the stool, turned away from him and was already busy with other things, saying, 'Well, then no matter. I'll give it to – '

'No, I'll take it,' Orlando said vehemently, scooping up the grey sweatshirt, which was pressed to his chest by the time she turned round to smile at him.

Orlando didn't want to lie to his mum. Thinking he might wear the college sweatshirt in bed with Shirley or if he was helping strip a car down, he found he was able to say, 'I will wear it, honest.' He was very strict about what he wore. How can you ever explain these things to your mum? He couldn't say, 'Mum, it's not that I don't *like* the top you bought me, it's more a case that the day I wear it will be the day I cease to have any self-respect; it will be when nothing matters anymore, when I've given up the ghost, and am myself in name only.'

The chamber and trigger-guard were at Shirley's. When she was out once, he'd super-glued them down the back of her radiator and never told her. He whistled through the letter-box (for only the policeman ever knocks), and let himself in.

Shirley's flat was like no one had moved in. At first, when you walked in you thought there was just the stack and the bed. And that was it. The stack was a top-of-the-range AIWA, the speakers right next to it and not spread out across the room. It looked like it had just been put there. In the kitchen there was still a bit of builder's or fitter's polythene stuck in the hinge of a cupboard. The cupboard was bare, save for loose teabags and half a packet of rice. The bed was a single mattress on the floor, covered with an Indian rug and some cushions. After a while you began to see other signs of habitation: wooden blinds on the windows, yesterday's chicken, sweetcorn and pepper curry combo in a glass bowl in the fridge. A mini Marcus Garvey parchment-style wall-hanging, that charcoal drawing of the sulky-but-cute Rasta kid.

In Shirley's flat, however, there was a sense which he'd only ever had once elsewhere at Warrington Station. The wrong train, the wrong scenery – was it two years ago? – and so he'd had to get off at this random, meaningless station. He'd crossed the mini-footbridge with its arabesque tags in marker pen, and a rusted NF scratched into the grey paint. ('Niggers Forever' as Shirley says.) He had stood in the pleasant, warm, fine drizzle, his mid-afternoon trance resting its focal length on one of those little boxes full of BR wiring away down the line. Some partisan railwayman had stencilled the name of a London team – A.F.C. or C.F.C. – on it. Orlando gradually became aware that no one in the world knew where he was. Every care left him, lifted from neck and shoulders, flesh and bone. He was shot of everything. He wasn't in any pattern no more. He took off his Walkman, listening to the dangling inner earpieces – the crazy soundtrack of that old and angry film he wasn't in – and started giggling. He rolled up to a kiosk which looked like a garden shed, and chatted to the man who sold papers there. The man was suspicious at first, but was soon infected by Orlando's excellent spirits, and started grinning broadly himself. From all his years inside the kiosk, watching the commuters, he could share Orlando's tone of detached outsider's amusement. Yes, it was an odd place to live when you look at it.

Orlando sauntered off with a token purchase of some gum. He strolled to the end of the platform past the red 'No Passengers Past This Point' sign made of tin and nailed to a post. He walked down the platform slope to the track and on to the coals. He stared at a wooden crate full to the brim with long-forgotten rusty wheel-pins, spent track brackets and exhausted couplings.

The train was on time and approached very slowly. Orlando regained the incline and walked back past the driver's cabin. The driver was staring at Orlando vexedly for being off limits. Orlando had, therefore, to stand right outside the window and stare back until the driver looked away. This the driver did with a testy rustle of the newspaper he returned to. Orlando moved off, and got on to the train. He was back on board.

Shirley came out of the bathroom wearing a faded

pink towelling bathrobe, a new grey towel wrapped in a turban round her head. He was sitting on the floor leaning his back against the wall, the knees of his long legs raised.

Outside, she usually wore her hair scraped back severely, tightly bound at the scalp in a top-knot. She often gelled down the pulled-back hair, lacquering it over her head. Only from the top-knot out could you see any of its natural curliness. Shirley rubbed her loose hair dry with the unravelled turban. As she rubbed, with her head tilted 180 degrees to the side, she looked at him through the damp, shaggy, hanging hair.

'What's up?'

No, he couldn't breathe a word. If he told her he'd sully the place. The side of his hand pushed the TV remote by tiny measures to and fro on the carpet.

'It's nothing.'

She straightened up with a widely arcing side-flick of her long black hair, and stood before him, hands on her hips.

He slowly raised his eyes to hers. 'What?' he asked her. She stared some more, blinked, then went back into the bathroom.

But the spirit of place he loved was gone anyway. His decision to withhold the full picture from Shirley had reduced her flat to a little fantasy island. It was now a theme-park of calm, rather than the principality of calm it had been before, due to the ease with which he and Shirley could be themselves when alone together here, and dispense with the thousand etiquettes and observancies of the neighbourhood.

She was telling him a tale of last night at the Ebo. He laughed at her characterisations and impressions of people they both knew; he appreciated the intelligence she gave him about who was standing with whom, or who was out of control – but some bar had come down, some invisible bar. He felt tetchy – both restless and tired, tense and whooped. And he felt like he was getting more tired and more restless all the time he was here.

They watched *Married With Children*, which had become an institution with them. Only they, it seemed, knew about this late-night sitcom. Tonight, though, it all seemed to Orlando like a too obviously unreal studio set. He could only see actors and camera angles, could only hear a studio audience and notice the US-quality videotape.

They bedded down on the mattress thinking they wouldn't make love that night. There was a charge between them, however, through having been so remote and formal all evening. Now he felt the smooth outside of her thigh touch the outside of his for an instant, as she got comfortable. He saw her breasts move mesmerically under the short T-shirt and her beloved arse and thighs as he got up again to turn off the hi-fi so its graphic equalizer lights didn't keep her awake. He crept up behind her so he was standing there when she turned round.

On the bed, he pushed her top up with the butt of his palm. When her shirt was over her face, he left it there as a joke. She was pretend-furious when she finally dragged it off her head, and punched him in the ribs, rolling on top of him. Her knees held a pillow down on his face. Facing south, she pushed down his shorts and pulled his T-shirt up over his skinny ribs. Sobs of muffled laughter came from under the anchored-down pillow. He cuffed her off him, and then they were making love half on and half off the mattress.

He felt the small of her back arching up out of the palm of his hand. Everything was all right with the world, when suddenly he was seeing what was before him as Buzz might see it: crass and low and mean and insidious and unimaginative and evil. Shirley's abandonment was something Orlando treasured without realising it. Now, ugh, he could only hear what he knew Buzz would make of it. 'See? Women are like dogs on heat. Look at that – *anyone* could touch her here and here and she'd jerk around just the same.'

Orlando argued back in his head. 'No, they *couldn't*. No one else could.' Hadn't it taken him and Shirley ages to get to this? That was what they had that was special, that they could be this open with one another. Shirley looked at his screwed-up face and took it to be the conventional fuck-face.

The estate was a small world looking inwards. In a small world your reputation can get about in a nighttime: she does this and this, and she'll let you do this. The girls on the estate were carefully fastidious. But to Orlando it was as if Buzz were standing in the room: 'No wonder they have to act so picky about who they fuck and don't, when this is what they can be reduced to.'

He lay on his back in the post-coital swoon with both his arms round her, heads leaning together. Evil may have fine-sprayed the empty flat, but that wasn't the whole story. He felt that what had saved him was that he was with Shirley, and not some ho he was just shagging.

Orlando had the whole gun bar the clip now. The clip was at his nan's. Her flat was over in Beasley. Even though he looks full-black, the only two grandparents still alive when he was born were white.

He went a long way round to get the bus. He'd get pressure if seen boarding a bus like a schoolie. At the other end – in the civilian zone – the bus-stop was right on his gran's front window. A row of cans and a knotted chip-paper had been left on her sill by people waiting for the bus. Orlando cleared the litter away like a mourner weeding a grave and let himself into her flat.

His nan was dying. Her cot had been moved into the front room so she could be near the telly and the big Calor gas heater. This also meant being near the thuddery bus-diesel trembling the pane, and the backsides sitting on the sill. She used to think the sill-perchers might fall through the glass. She'd worry whether she'd survive the impact if they fell on top of her. Would the net curtains catch the glass?

He was shocked when he saw her there. She was with her toothless neighbour, who soon left. He sat down and held his nan's amphibian hand in his own. The translucent skin was like ET's in that scene by the river with the vole sniffing round, or like an uncooked chicken. She used to wear one of those copper anti-arthritis bracelets. That was gone now, just like the bands or clips which used to hold her white hair up, all the things which bound her here. This was the first time he'd seen her white hair down like a girl's. It was almost indecent. The white shoulder-length hair, though thinned right out in one or two bald places, was quite beautiful and eerily clean.

Still holding her mini-mitt in his hand, he sat on the arm of the armchair by the head of the cot. She lay on her side. He couldn't be sure that she recognised him. She only ever intermittently registered him, and that was when he shook her hand around so fast that he was almost doing a macabre handjive with her. But she wasn't completely out of it. Something was occupying her, keeping her pupils small and sharp in the stagnant pond. She was intent on something invisible fifty yards away. She was moving her jaw as if talking, or as if, thought Orlando, mouthing words called to her across some distance, trying to make them out.

She closed her eyes, and Orlando listened to his Nana's scraping breaths. Here, dear reader, were one of the last still-working pairs of pre-Henry Ford, nineteenth-century lungs, grinding down at last, noisy as old Victorian machinery. She'd been making this last-gasp racket outside Death's door not for days, but weeks. A sound something like when the big, six-foot aluminium bins by each stairwell on the estate were dragged across the concrete to the big yellow iron hook of the loader. He listened to her scraping lungs; each one sounded like this would be her last breath on earth. Horrifyingly, every now and then she wouldn't

99

breathe at all, or if she did it made no sound. She was gone. This would be good for the eyes. And then, like a musical reprise, came the dragging concrete sound, the aluminium bins, and under the threadbare dressing-gown the lungs pull up and out again for the eighty-killionth time in a row. The last generation to scrub doorsteps were the last of the tough old duellers with death.

As Orlando held her hand the mask of street smarts melted. (Maybe melted by the full-on Calor gas heater. It had 'Miser', 'Economy', 'Pensioner In Winter' and 'Dying Pensioner In Winter' settings.) At first the hard self-possessed look only gave way to another type of self-consciousness: all tremulous and palpitating, more with desire for the Big Spiritual Experience than concern for her. This passed and he changed the hand that held hers (his palm was getting a bit clammy). He listened to the bus and fantasised about going and shocking the sill-perchers with the gun and extreme violence.

Suddenly Nana raised herself up. She reached out to some vision beyond the Texaco garage. What was she seeing? She nudged him aside like he was in the way of this vision. He felt slighted. He felt he should remind her he was here, and imposed himself back on her consciousness. She shook her bent finger at him. She squeezed his hand a couple of times as if to say, 'thanks, but not now', and shockingly raised herself up again to see whatever the vision was. She was holding her arms out to the vision, too, and making a noise, again rather like ET – just as longing but more gravelly and louder, more like mooing. This repeated itself several times; each time Orlando intervened, and got her benign 'not you' gestures.

Who knows what she saw? Old friends? Grandpop? Her childhood home now open again? Angels? She fell back again. Had Orlando seen the death rattle? She just went back to sleep, stone-grinding away louder than ever.

He got up. He went to the chipped drawer of the kidney-shaped mahogany dresser. The clip was there. Still inside the soft plastic pencil case he'd had as a kid at school. He felt its uncompromising hard edges through the soft plastic. He didn't get the clip out to look at it. It seemed to be buzzing with evil. He took his hand off the plastic, shut the drawer and left it there.

Now he was wondering what to do. After only a few minutes the neighbour flicked the letter-box once, and came in. Usually he hated this old bag for her greasy, all-day nightie and for not putting her teeth in. But now he was glad of her.

'Thanks for looking after our nan,' he said.

Outside there was no one waiting for the bus. He walked down the street. A light wind drummed an empty plastic bottle against the metal brim of a litter-bin. Bits of chilly sun reflected brightly off old shards of finely broken glass in the road. Across the street he saw a stocky white boy. He was about twenty-two with short gingery-brown hair. He was doing that walk they all did: a walk which tells the world how much pain you can give out. The aggressive strut that says 'don't mess'. It struck Orlando as ugly and absurd. Mad.

Orlando realised he had always hated nastiness. He

thought of Lyndon Thomas. Everyone liked him. He was peaceful, with his ten-speed racer, which he'd smilingly lift into the hall of his house. He was a Tai Kwon Do champion, but never in any trouble, never dragged into the whole grisly plot. His neutrality wasn't resented as neutrality usually is. And when he let on to you crossing the street you felt good. He was like a community leader. He'd done this or that in the riots or when that girl was run over by joy-riders. Orlando remembered seeing him once when there was a fire somewhere on Souvraney. The blaze chucked up unfeasible amounts of black smoke all afternoon, which the white firemen could not quell. He remembered Lyndon Thomas walking across the road, lined-face grinning, saying to the gathered crowd without breaking his pace: 'And *we* can't get a job . . .' He wasn't in crime, and he didn't pack a piece, maybe he could be him.

Friday night and feeling absolved, he stands, orange juice in hand, outside the red-brick wall of the Mower. Shirley is talking to some friends of hers a little way away. Half-eleven on a dry, warm, close night.

Across the street, two yellow streetwasher trucks back up very slowly. They are spraying water over the road and gutter. Orange sirens spin silently on top of the trucks. There's a chlorine tang in the nostrils. The water they slooshed down has dispelled the whole atmosphere of the street. Just a few moments ago it was all dusty, airless. Now, the city's night-charge of adrenalin, pheremones and fear has been dispelled. The chemical air breathes clear and lifted; the fresh, wet streets are shiny and black. They've wiped the slate clean. A new start.

Backwards they go, slow as the minute hand they're turning back, slow so as not to miss any of the mistakes we want undone, brave municipal yellow streetwasher trucks reversing at night. It can all be different now, thinks Orlando. His gaze rests on the sluicing undercarriages of the noisy trucks. He is in one of those bug-eyed middle-distance trances you fall into when standing under a shelter when it rains.

Methodical and gestatively slow, the street-soaker trucks reverse. Whew, it does the heart good to smell wet streets on a dry night.

Two figures come out from between the trucks in silhouette, moving fast. One of them is holding something. A brown paper bag. The next sweep of yellow light shows a puggy half of Balcony Watchman's face. Too late. He swings the brown paper bag hard at Orlando's hip. The axe he is holding inside the bag splits Orlando's hip-joint. Orlando slams to the ground faster than the swing of the arm that dropped him.

The other man, the white man, his short hair in a widow's peak, knocks Shirley out cold with a punch in the throat. Balcony Watchman drags shrieking Orlando into a car.

The gear sounds too high to Orlando as they drive through upside-down streets. Lying on his back, he sees eaves and upper-storey windows stop and start. The familiar made strange by agony. The gear drops and there's a new sound. His drivers are laughing because the Espace they stole in good faith has turned out to be a spasmobile. They make mongy noises and parody disabled driving. They career over the empty roads in unexpected swerves which drive blinding pain up through Orlando from his severed hip. As he blacks out, his last thought is that his nan will outlive him.

Eight
LEVITY _____

Hup! Back again, Kenny. The rest of the crew were all up on deck when I nipped out. Alone with the big speaker-sound booming in the hull, I grazed on left-over tucker, finished off half finished glasses of wine, the odd bottle of spirits. Quite a bit of wine as it goes. Where were we? Yes. The balance between past and present . . .

When we're very powerfully attracted to someone, is it that ole devil called love? Or is it that other ole devil called unfinished psychological business?

The first time I ever saw Svetlana was on *International Athletics*, and do you know what? I had to turn the fucking telly off. Whenever I saw her on the box subsequently – Europeans, Gateshead, World Championships (I had – whaddyaknow – become something of an afficianado of the women's high jump event) – it was the same thing. What was it that troubled me so, dear hillbilly? What had I *seen*?

Whatever it was, it bothered me totally. My atoms were in disarray. I was in hormonal panic. Upset, cross, grumpy, bewitched, bothered and bewildered. And it was like this from the very first time I saw her. Pictures coming live from Helsinki . . .

The evening is darker there than here, the lighting more dramatic. She is standing – Freudians, prepare to throw your caps in the air – on a rostrum. There was a moment's delay before she got her silver-place flowers, last. Last because the official was going from right to left with the flowers – bronze, gold, silver. Still smiling, still looking out once or twice towards the instamatic flashbulbs of the shadowy crowd. But, for a second, I dunno – some doubt? I was jealous of the Burgermeister's lascivious, stinking, inaudible comments mouthed to her. (She smiled throughout, bearing up well.) I was jealous of the view he – no doubt – tried to sneak down her track-suit-zippered cleavage as she stooped to his portly, bald, grossly smiling figure for her well-earned medal. Bravo Romania! I felt he was less attentive with the bronze-placed, bronzed Cuban, but that might just have been me.

And I don't meant libidinously troubled, either. It *wasn't* lust, Mr Rogers. Let me stress that, just in case you're handing this letter round a smutty, redneck pool hall. No. More text-book-beautiful jumpers had come and gone that day eliciting only the usual cry of woe. (The Swedish newcomer, the clattering French-woman . . .) Let me also say that I do *not* believe in love at first sight. But I do believe that from the moment I saw her, I somewhere knew all the things about us that I'm only just now piecing together.

But must it always be a dark, fatalistic impulse? *L'abîme appelle l'abîme.* Or, as the psychologists say, Mr Abuser marries Mrs Abusee. In so many Updike–Bellow passages, the state of attraction is the fatal mistake, the vain folly that you have to keep paying and paying for. Are they right? Every time you 'go with your heart,' must it lead to some ghastly _Play For Today_ hell? Do the lyrics of ABC really count for nothing in the real world? ('Look Of Love' now playing.) The real world, that is, of Martin Fry's Hodgkin's disease? I dunno, but here's a quote from my toilet-reading . . .

> Why should we bother about the possible existence of a force equal and opposite to gravity? Could we not leave all such questions for the experts to quarrel over on their own recondite level? The answer is an unequivocal 'No'. The whole world has accepted Newton's concept of gravity as an unopposed force and it now enters into every aspect of our thinking and feeling . . . [it] is a pulling-down concept; it heavies everything. The notion of 'upwardness' being a living response as primary as gravity no longer enters the human mind. The _OED_, for instance, says loftily of levity: 'In pre-scientific physics, regarded as a positive property inherent in different degrees, in virtue of which [bodies] tend to rise . . . obsolete except historically or allusively.' Another magisterial door-slam. Yet if we look in the right direction, evidence for the existence of levity is as clear . . . in our everyday experience as . . . gravity.'
>
> _Gravity and Levity_, Alan McGlashan

And an illustration from my toilet life . . .

107

By 5 a.m. of the Mexican dawn of me and Svetlana's holiday in hell, I knew I'd have to do it now. Felt I'd regret any note, and didn't have the confidence to put anything in writing.

I walked out into the sea, pleasantly drunk. Still, alas, thinking 'Oh – I hope I get the Big Tolstoyan Stuff that goes with this one.' Walked into the water as far as I could walk. Smiling and singing meaningless, subtext-free songs, songs that were good for singing. We'd been at a dance earlier, and my head was still buzzing and humming.

When I could no longer reach the bottom, I struck out for death. Front crawl at first, then on my back floating, getting my breath back, gurgling and humming. Rolled over happily, luxuriously, flopping over to front crawl again for another five minutes or so.

Another breather. I looked back at the lights on the beach. Green and yellow. They could have been anywhere or anyone's. As it happened they were still the lights of our resort, 'Fantasy Island'. This far from shore – a mile? Two miles? – I slipped off my long trunks. 'We came into this world with nothing, and it is sure we go out of this world with nothing.' Felt I should be enjoying the tropical night, the last vista, and so did some breast-stroke and doggy-paddle while looking around. Then I did the lazy-man, half-on-your-side stroke that my dad did when I went to an outdoor pool with him on a campsite when I was seven. This was how grown-men swim. A deep breath and I ploughed on with front crawl. Sudden surges of anger took me forward each time I felt my balls about to bust with effort. On, on, on – the tireder I am, the less I'll feel when I drown. The more puffed I am, the less of a ghastly fight in the salty airlock it'll be. Maybe I've got ten more strokes in me. Seven – eight – nine – when I got to ten I re-doubled my gasping efforts. Let me be further out so there's no going back, no mistake.

The light of the day I'd never see had come up, and before long there might be shipping. I gashed my stomach on some jagged, carbuncley reef. The blood was immediate and thin. I was – oddly in the circumstances – frightened of sharks. Oh dear, here was a high reef which I would have to clamber over, cutting arms, and arse a bit – but, most thoroughly, hands and feet. Deep gashes here, and the one on my feet still hurts as I write to you. I was now walking on the coral, the coral reef having shelved up completely to form a raised islet three miles out. It must have looked like I was walking on water as I stood exposed on the razor reef, but I felt like an Indian walking over hot coals who hasn't meditated enough.

The dry wind blew about my gooseflesh. Painfully, painfully, two yards a minute, I tried all positions to find the way of least gashes and stabs: all-fours; crablike with feet-first; crab-like with feet-first and sobbing; standing up again and stepping gingerly from painful thing to painful thing; checking with hand on each jagged rock, and then stepping; thinking about how much I hate myself and then trying to 'welcome' the pain. (How soon one's nameless, Gestalt guilt and self-loathing evaporate when you put them to it!)

At last I was over the reef. Mean stegosaurus-backed coral and odd stinging-things gave way to a patch of soft sand. And then a deeper one, and then another. I walked on. The water was now up to my stinging ankles, then bloody shins, then sore thighs. Now we're getting somewhere. The wind blew around my noisy ears, shivering my gashed and pulpy flesh. My skin was just starting to sting and ache. I'm all fucked-up. There's only straight-on death now anyway. I felt like the still-crawling wreckage of Arnie at the end of *T2*. Deep breath. Let's get this fucking *over* with. Walked forward fast into the deepening water until my feet could no longer touch the bottom.

The final plunge. I dived down, but floated to the top again before I was out of breath. Deep breath, and dived down again with eyes open. I saw two white pillars of rock on the sea bed. I swam down to anchor myself there, while the last bubbles of life left my stupid lungs. My hand sent a flurry of sea-bed sand up just before I reached the two rocky columns, but I still managed to grab them blind. They were more slippy than I'd imagined. They moved back suddenly. I hung on. They stopped. I looked up and saw that I was holding someone's legs. I stood up and was face to face with a large, sixty-year-old German woman, her face cross under a rubber swimming cap. She raised her hands while stepping back fast, making loud Brünhilde-type noises.

A large pink neon sign read 'PLEASURE BEACH'. The steeply shelving sand lifted me suddenly to the shore as if I were standing on the back of a surfacing sea-mammal. Out on the clumsy, surfless sand, however, I knew the helpless indecent exposure of a

beach-donkey. Foreign parents gesticulated affront-
edly at me, as they shepherded their children away.
Clip-clopped through them all, head-down, keeping
to the straight beach-donkey line. When I had gained
the sparse palm-trees. I swiped an unattended beach
towel.

Straight on brought me to a strange hotel's foyer.
The Toyota Hire stand confirmed this wasn't heaven.
On the courtesy phone, in a formal tone, I ordered a
cab. I sat down in a cool leather armchair, as decently
towelled as any other immodest European. Merciful
heaven sent no hot pursuers from the Rhadamanthine
beach.

I stared at the guppies, groupers or rock dobies in
the fish-tank, at the self-pity of the down-turned
mouths and protruding bottom lips. 'You were nearly
in here with us,' their looks said, 'suspended in
aquatic self-pity.' Yeah, I felt like the Man from
Atlantis. He was in *Dallas*, wasn't he? Parents shot;
Bobby (?) Ewing, how inappropriate a thought, Billy?
Real-life parents shot. Did the gunmen know it was
them? Who they were? Was that –

'You wanna cab?' said the Mexican. He made it
sound like he was hustling a fare, not answering a
call-out.

'Oh, hi. Are you the cab I ordered?'

He did a *no comprendez* blink. 'You wanna cab?'

'Fantasy Island?'

'Si,' he said, impatiently. He looked like he was
representing macho in a carnival parade or pageant.
Tooled cowboy boots, too-tight jeans, overweight in a
tight T-shirt with an unlaced lace-up neck, a kerchief
round his neck, Big O-type shades.

After a short while, his brow cleared itself of what-ever business at home or at work had been vexing him over the first few kilometres. He looked in the rear-view mirror and grinned. A gold-tooth or two. He looked at the right-hand-side road and then the rear-view again: time for today's comic distraction.

'You swim from Fantasy Island?'

At this point (still being me – just), I did of course want the Big Poetic Moment. The Stranger As Soothsayer. Two Cultures United By The Universal. The Meaningful Dialogue In Broken English. I was also anxious to establish heterosexual credentials. Here was me in a towelling skirt, being driven down a strange lane. The driver, for all I knew, could be the geezer from *The Comfort Of Strangers*. 'That sort of thing is quite common,' says that book's Chief Of Police, as I remember.

'Women make you do crazy things,' I said with the spastic jocularity of the hopefully 'international' quip.

'Eh?'

'She makes me mad.'

The Grand Poetic Dialogue of Meaningful Ex-change was surely only around the corner of this hotting-up asphalt, with its little landslides in the road here and there. An intuitive peasant-savant simplifica-tion here, a platitude there, and before you know it, *BOOM!* Act V – I'm elevated into resolution, and all the love the soundtrack has to give is mine. The host of unseen witnesses in the clouds show themselves. I'm not alone.

He indicated my grazes and wounds by waving his fingers up and down the front of his too-tight T-shirt. 'She did that to you?'

'Not this morning, no.'

His high-tar cackle reminded me of the metallic, cylindrical cigar holder I'd seen in his breast pocket in the foyer. The hotel fish-tank's guppies or rock gobies would have been hardly less surprised to find a smile on their faces than I was now. After a while he turned on Radio Mexico. I had, it appeared, lived to hear Country 'n' Western sung in Spanish.

When I got back she was still asleep. When she woke up I was still asleep. When I woke up she complained about the blood on the bathroom floor and told me that the maid might not clean it up because of the AIDS scare.

I only ever tried this once before. Just before I met her. Here's the diary entry:

Last night was meant to be my last night. I'm still here.

The woods – off an A-road off a slip-road somewhere in the wet night. Temazepam, Anafranil, Paracetamol, Stolichnaya. Broke off a stick my own height and stuck it in the ground as a flagpole. Tied on a pillowcase as a white flag: you win, I surrender.

Cried – and that at least has been for the last time. Stopped. There, I'd emptied out the drops of water, like a milk bottle rinsed and shaken out for doorstep return. All done. Closed my eyes and listened to the dripping woods, the windy white noise trees. At last some rain on this muggy, muggy day. Listened to the purring pills in the vodka. Plink, plink, plink, plonk, plink, kerrplunk-plonk, *plink-plink-FIZZZ*.

Lay down after the first swig. I'm tired and I want

to go to bed. Flagpole at my head like a dead dog's cross of twigs. The black foam earphones of the Walkman warmed my damp ears while I listened to 'I Know It's Over'. It's perfect. He never sang anything better. Another swig of the special brew. The end of the song. I took off the headphones. A voice. Two voices.

'HELP! GET OFF! Please don't. I'll give you money. PLEASE, please. Please. Please please.'

The second voice had the irritated lethargy of a white-trash dad disturbed by his common-law wife's crying tot: 'Shut up, you're *dead*. It's over. You are dead. Just shut the fuck up.'

I raised my head, and saw a man pull out a butcher's gutting knife with bloodsoaked string wound around the handle.

'Do him in the head now, just there,' said another figure I hadn't noticed before. These were the most horrible words I'd ever heard.

And then, what do you know, here's a rum thing, I appear to be moseying over towards the commotion. Why, I'm practically on top of them. They still don't see me. I'll have to speak.

'Let him go.'

They looked up, shocked. They're not to know I'm just a coward they'd disturbed on his way out. I'm so calm – *plink-plink-fizz!* – so sure. I've got all the time in the world. Shall we stand staring all night? Yes, why not? I am as un-psyche-out-able as Ghandi practising his civil-disobedience-look in the mirror at the end of a good sewing day.

They look like they're bitterly calculating some-thing, and then they run.

They leave a bleeding man lying on the ground. I pinch the wounds together. Oh, but what's wound and what's not in all this mess? I drag the pillowcase off the green, powdery stick. I rip it, but it isn't quite the Kildare half-and-half I am after. This makes it difficult to knot behind his back. So I shout at him to hold it in place if it slips. I put one of his arms over my neck because that's the thing to do. But I'm sure this, in raising his ribs, is actually causing him more pain. But this is the 'Nam hobble, and anyway, there's the Saab. Laid him on the back seat of the car I'd hoped I'd seen the last of.

'What's your name, mate?' I ask, back on the slip road.

'Orlando.' And then, 'What's yours?'

'Kevin.'

'Kevin, could you drive a bit more carefully, please?'

BOOK II

One
ROGUE FEMALE ⸻

Of all the people in the Rose Cottage that night, only Karen Doonan had seen the whole thing. She alone had watched him come in right from the door, and so had seen the incident rather than the fracas. There may have been other witnesses, for when the police got to the Cottage, they didn't seal off the area, didn't take statements there and then, except for the barstaff and someone with a nosebleed. Either way, Karen Doonan would be the star witness.

One of her old flatmates from her last bolt-hole in Archway phoned, and told her the police had been round. Karen had shared a flat in Archway with seven others. She had got on best with Jim and Anna, and the three of them had found the flat in Somerstown together. Thank fuck she'd moved, she thought. The police must have found her through the tax she was paying at the restaurant. They must have gone there and the restaurant gave them her home address. Well, she wasn't paying tax in her new job. Was there any way they could find her now? They'd been to see Mark's mum, but Mark's mum didn't know where she lived.

This was a long shot by the police. Even though,

psychologically, it felt like they were right on her, she knew that in reality they had run aground. This flat in Somerstown, where she lived with Jim and Anna, was the longest she'd lived anywhere since she'd been on the run. She liked it there and she wasn't going to move again.

She was working in the office of a computer magazine, answering the phones. Here was everybody else, with all their interconnecting lives, and here was she. She felt unpleasantly like a spy in a foreign country, a sleeper acquiring a fast familiarity with alien names of the office, pretending an interest in the incoming calls.

'Hello, Matrix.'

'Karen?'

'Oh hi, Anna.'

'The police have just been here.'

A creeping, loathsome coldness covered Karen's whole skin: back, belly, arms, legs, cheeks, neck. Her stomach felt full of industrial effluence. There they'd stood, perhaps even in her own room. Reality.

'How did they get my address?'

'The landlady at Archway had a forwarding address for me and Jim, and guessed you came with us. What are you gonna do?'

The police had come down to London on the train that day. They had left an 061- number with Anna. Karen looked around the office: unfamiliar people whose first names she knew. She felt like her life here was just so much location-hunting. The whole thing looked like a tableau from which she might be re-moved without much notice. It was all very distant. A man went to get a paper cup of water from a plastic dispenser, which looked like an upside-down, bloated Evian bottle. He shared a joke with a female colleague who was walking by, and Karen watched her go out the door, into the corridor, and disappear. The job had been a bit boring, but suddenly she loved the key-boards and terminals, and the brightly-coloured graphics lying on desks, and the old fellas in overalls delivering boxes that needed to be signed for. She was about to be zapped out of this easy film set.

On the desk nearest to her, a dark, olive-skinned girl with a bob was looking down and frowning un-happily over something on her empty desk. It was a letter, perhaps nothing to do with work. Karen picked up one of the purple phones on the three-phone con-sole before her, on which none of the lights were flashing.

She was put through to a man who had been wait-ing for her call for a year.

He controlled his excitement. 'Hello Karen, my name's Tony.'

'I don't want to come in.'

'Yes, I understand, and we know why. The thing is this: if he goes down, then you'll have nothing to worry about. He's of no use to the gang then, and it's simple economics – there's no money in a contract once he's already been put away where he belongs. And you know that's where he belongs, don't you, Karen?'

'Yes, but what if he isn't? What if he's not put away?

It's easy for you to say, "Oh, he probably will be," but if he's not, then I've had it.'

'If you testify, he will be; and if you don't, he won't – plus if he's not, you know you'll never be able to come back home.'

'Look, I've lasted this far,' she said, but the words died on her in the saying.

'We know where you live, Karen. We were there today. There's a warrant out for your arrest. That shouldn't be the way you come in. That would be wrong; I don't want to do it that way, and there's no need to do it that way.' It was as though he had read her mind with his next sentence: 'We've put a hold on the ports. There's nowhere left to go, Karen. We'll look after you, we can put you in a hotel under a false name. I will personally pick you up and take you to the court. Whenever you need me, I'm totally here for you. I've no other cases to attend to . . .'

'Look, I need to think about this. I can't just decide now. What's your name, so I can ask for you again?'

'It's DC Jones. But just ask for Tony. I'm the only Tony here. Well, there is another one, but he has to be called Anthony, ha ha.'

'You won.'

'I won.'

'I'm not saying "yes" yet. I've got to talk to people, and I've still got to think about it.'

When she had first moved to Somerstown a year ago, she had gone to a firm of solicitors whose ad Anna had seen in the *Camden Journal*: a small, two-roomed office, white walls and self-assembly desks. The solicitor there was in her mid-twenties, sunny with DM shoes and a silk dress with big green polka dots.

'Oh hi, you were meant to see Adrian, weren't you? I'm afraid he's been called out,' she had said that day, on which she had confirmed the Rosewood & Co. advice. She too had waived the fee when Karen mentioned it.

As the trial date got nearer and nearer, Karen had phoned this woman – Amanda – with other questions. Was she right in thinking that that would be that if she just made it to the day undetected? Was she doing the right thing? Or was she wrong in not testifying?

Now, a year later, the weather was exactly the same, Karen remembered, as when she'd turned into the street a year ago. The woman was wearing the same dress, as well, but with brown side-buckle shoes this time.

The advice was different, too. 'They've got this far; they've put a warrant out for your arrest. They obviously want you to go and testify. They're not going to stop. They're only a step away from getting hold of you, and the deal is you could wind up in prison.'

Karen went into the other office, which was empty (Adrian being absent again). 'If I don't go and they catch me,' she thought, 'and he does get let off and I have to spend thirty days in prison – fuck. Me sitting in jail whilst he's swanning around? *No.*' 'No,' she said out loud, finished one of absent Adrian's fags, and walked through.

The solicitor sat behind absent Adrian's desk. Instead of picking up the receiver, she dialled on speakerphone. Karen could hear the phone ringing on DC Jones's desk.

'I've got Karen Doonan here. My client is willing to come in.' During the call the woman folded her arms, pushed her chin forward and stared at an upright lighter. 'She is going to come in, but I'm looking after her, and I want assurances that if anything goes wrong you're going to provide safe houses and protection.' At the end of fifteen minutes' successful negotiations, she neatly laid the lighter on its side.

───────────────

INTERIOR. *NELLIE.* NIGHT.

KAREN: And I felt safe then, once I knew that they couldn't go back on that. Because if *I'd* have said it to them it wouldn't have made any shit at all.

───────────────

Walking from Camden to Euston, she cut through a small park. Ahead of her two swallows were behaving strangely. One of them seemed to be shivering. It was ruffling its feathers to keep itself warm, wrapping its wings around itself, its beak chattering. The bird appeared to have no appetite for the slimy pile of juicy pink worms which lay exhumed on the mud-casts beside it. Unusually it had retracted its feet and was resting its belly on the grass, rocking slightly. The other swallow was more energetic. On the bench nearby, it had found a pensioner in a velvet hat. The bird appeared to be stroking the old woman's hat with its smooth head, cooing and billing, while the pensioner tried to bat it away.

It was arranged that three plain-clothes policemen would meet her off the 10:50 at Manchester Piccadilly. As she got off the train it suddenly occurred to her that she didn't know what they looked like. She looked up to the end of the long grey platform. At the barrier, she saw them. They were so bad at looking casual she started laughing. They weren't blending in. If they'd been background extras in a film, Coppola, viewing it on his laptop monitor, would've come charging on to the concourse shouting, 'Who are those fucking guys in the background?'

'No,' she thought, 'I can't go out laughing.' After a year in hell it would have been wrong. She turned round, went back and joined the longer queue. From the back of the queue, she looked at them once more and started laughing again. One of them had his jacket over his shoulder. His pose was like those photos on the pillars at C&A (a model, some rocks, a stream). Another cop had some aviator shades on and even had a paper under his arm. DC Jones leant his forearms on the scraped blue metal of the ticket barrier, but he was much too tall for the attitude to seem natural. He tried to remedy this by poking a polished brogue through the blue metal rails so he could rest on it. This put him in such an unlikely posture that

125

passers-by were, he feared, liable to ask, 'Is your foot stuck?' Or, worse still, 'Is your foot stuck, officer?'

An electric truck sweeping litter reversed past the queue with a flashing orange light, obscuring them for long enough for her to recover her features. When she came out through the barrier she was beaming as she walked straight towards them.

Two
ASCENSION DAY ⸻

The high jump, Kenny, is one of those track-and-field events which still has an echo of conjecture about it, of Ancient Greek philosophical rumination made flesh. 'You think it possible, Demosthenes?' This echo of Ancient Greek speculation about the extreme limits of human fortitude is something it shares with the hundred metres, the decathlon, and the Platonic relationship.

I loved to watch her jump. Standing in the cavernous shade of the Oslo stadium's tunnel, wearing my laminate, or 'PASS' sticker, I used to try and look enigmatic, hoping people would think I was a five-thousand-metre genius who'd been injured out, but who had been awarded security clearance in honour of all the records I *would* have broken.

Standing in the shadow, I watch as she bends and peels off first one then a second layer of track suit. And there are the smooth, naked legs, the bare arms. Heart beating fast, adrenalin pumping – hers too, probably. Boom! Boom! A fourteen-year-old minion holds at arm's length a blue plastic basket for her to put the still-warm fabric in. The girl walks off, carrying the blue basket of Svetlana's clothes before her with a ceremonial manner. Where to? There was something clinical or institutional about these individual plastic trays of clothing. Then again, this was perfectly-working, self-cleansing, fully-functional, socialist Norway. Perhaps her clothes were taken down to nearby well-cared-for psychiatric patients. Here, star-crossed, lust-ridden, gibbering wrecks were briefly suffered to bury their convalescent faces in each tray of warm garments, to sob and to howl.

Svetlana, two - bits - of - thin - clothing - from - being - naked-before-millions, stretched and shook out her long legs, adjusted the absurdly random number on her woman's ribcage. Representing Romania, but speaking better English than Romanian (and neither like a native).

She smiled an open and friendly smile to a competitor. The frowning, graceless, petulant, self-important American smiled a disingenuous, careerist smile back – she thought she was being psyched-out.

A huge Canadian male, his slobby arse unseemly in lycra, vented his frustration on the shot-put. He'd probably been at lots of events she'd been at, by the look of all the comfort eating he'd done. The shot he threw was the smelted-down black lava of my belly. The noise he made when he threw the fucker was the noise I wanted to make half-way through every row I ever had with Svetlana. Just be fucking *moved* by me, woman. Just be swayed by what I say. Just let me have some effect, I'd think, as she sat, smiling across the cafe table, enjoying her own immovability.

She was on the runway. Commentators love to have their angle, their handle - the athlete's idiosyncracy is often all that stands between commentator and nationalist cliché. The commentators always went on and on about the fact that Svetlana Braila (ROM) had a long run-up, which started right out on the running track. (What a card! What a character! Crazy, just crazy!)

She waited in a force-field of preoccupation, while a gaggle of men from all over the world tried to impress her by running as fast as they could. They passed her by. She stepped back over the curving kerb on to the tartan track. A pause.

And who knows what gremlins of the mind make the high-jumper fail? Do guilt and the will to fail, babble in her ear, bubbling up over the clear line of concentration? There she stands, clearing her thoughts of the negative, concentrating on the technical, the specific, the actual.

In the distance, frantic, jostling men hurried to get back round to where she was again. The runners passed a grey-haired man in a blazer. He, in turn, had chosen a little brass bell to attract her attention. Ding! Ding!

The cracking-up tannoy operative, for his part, was to be heard trying to strike up a conversation with her in Norwegian. He seemed to trail off half-way, shrivelled by her lack of interest. Her concentration was pure, staring at the high-jump bar. A little later the tannoy man tried again in French, the language of lovers, to no avail. By now he sounded resigned to a lifetime of formalities: a parked car blocking an exit, a reminder, a regret.

The crowd broke into spontaneous applause as she hooked her blue shorts back down over her buttocks. Many of them rose to their feet, much to the chagrin, I'd expect, of the Norwegian shot-putter who had just broken a world record.

The runners finished. They were panting with hands on hips, or bent over with their hands on their knees, some squatting, head bowed.

Above them, the fifty-foot-high electronic screen showed the Norwegian shot-putter's throw again (for those who may have missed it). Suddenly and shockingly it changed. There was something alarming about seeing her face writ so large. I felt exposed, and guilty of the thoughts I had.

Making wings of her elbows she was off and running. I knew she knew she wasn't going to do it. She was charging a bit; there was a gravel sound before she jumped.

She was well clear. Her arcing back was levelling out high up. Her arms spreadeagled and floppy as if falling; her soaraway shorts. When she seemed to be in the clear, her cantilever ankle brought the dayglo bendy-bar tumbling after. She ended up curled in a ball upside-down, kind of on her neck. She stayed like that without moving on the deep, slumberdown crash-mat. Two seconds, three seconds. And then (as if aware of the eyes on her haunches?) she flicked herself back with her hands in a backwards roll, stood up elegantly, and walked off the crash mat.

Oh no, I was a jinx. I bet Otto or Freddie or Shitface or Dicksweat were good luck to her. Was I dragging her down? I watched her studying the ground, biting her lip. At that moment she looked more like a coach or manageress than athlete. Had she started thinking it was me that was dragging her down? Was the leaden weight of our holiday in hell weighing upon her? The men in blazers put the bar back up, and stood either side like doormen.

Three
WITNESSES _____

'Just to explain a few things about the court procedure, Karen . . . ' DC Tony Jones was about six-foot-four, rugby player build. They stood in the white marble corridor outside court number eleven of the Crown Court. As he spoke, his usual everything's-under-control bass monotone was tempered by an over-casual matter-of-factness, while the other policemen moved away. 'What'll happen is we'll wait here with you until you're called – hopefully that'll be today. At the end of the corridor there's the witness support group where you can go and have a coffee or a cup of tea and a chat. They're very helpful. When you go into court, you'll be led straight to the witness box – if you want to have a look around when the court's adjourned you can. The first person who'll address you will be the usher who'll swear you in, then the crown. He's conducting his own defence. The layout of the court room is – '

'*What* did you say?'

'He's conducting his own defence,' said Tony Jones, in a straight voice now, looking her in the eyes.

'You never told me that!'

'We didn't think you'd show up if we did.'

'Too bloody right I wouldn't!'

Small, asthmatic, chemically haunted by her miscarriage, a grey haired bottle-blonde, ground down by a year in hiding, a year cut off from home and friends, menstrually challenged, bits of dead hair in her hairgrips, fibres on her clothes from the frazzled sleeves of her last T-shirts . . . and now, what was always going to be very bad was going to be much worse.

'Oh fuck,' she said, looking up and down the corridor in panic, tutting.

The witness is totally alone. You're not allowed to talk about the case to anyone, not even to the witness support group. If someone heard you, they could get a mis-trial. And someone might.

Members of Buzz's family had stationed themselves in the witness support room, hoping to get stuff on the witnesses: where they were going out that night, an address, a mis-trial. Karen assumed this huddle were other witnesses, and so nodded a hello, and gave them a supportive grin whenever she walked in or stood beside them at the coffee-urn.

The witness is not allowed in the courtroom to hear other witnesses. Some of the witnesses were faces she knew, others she'd never seen before, even though they must have been in the pub that night. Everyone was as isolated as on the day of the Last Judgement. As isolated as that bit at the beginning of *Camberwick Green*, when whichever character was central to that week's story revolved up out of the metal music box, like statues of themselves. The puppets always looked oddly melancholy in coming out of that box, be it Dr Mopp or Windy Miller. Their friendly features were unprepared for that scene's hard message: 'We live, as we die: *alone*, children.'

In the corridor she nodded as Jimmy Beck went in. She knew him from the Rose Cottage and around. He was handsome, mixed-race and with shoulder-length locks. He smiled back at Karen, showing his variegated teeth.

Jimmy Beck was part of the Wythenshawe crowd who had always lived by a policy that you don't grass. He was a dealer with previous himself, and yet here he was testifying because he had thought, 'No. What Buzz did was wrong.' Was this nineteen-year-old, whom she didn't know, walking past her in the corridor, doing the same thing? she wondered.

The black kid's short hair was unkempt. Here and there scruffy twists grew longer than the rest. His walking stick had no rubber tip and made a loud noise in the marble corridor. His dry face seemed too tired for his age, which showed in his slenderness, and in that vague look of mild shock the young have. His eyes met hers for a second, but neither recognised the other, and he looked away. At first, Karen had thought his dead stare was that of a gang-member, but when their eyes met, she saw that it was the wrong sort of hard. It was a broken-spirit hard, a defeated, hopeless, bitter hard – and, crucially, the hard eyes of someone you might still pick on if you didn't have a heart.

He wore school-type charcoal-coloured trousers. On his grey sweatshirt were stains of oil – or was it Marmite? – which seemed to make more remote the never-never land of the legend: 'ORLANDO HIGH'.

He ticked down the long, shadowy marble corridor, and when he had turned the corner she could still hear the stick.

Due to all the times the judge had had to clear the court, and due to all the mad perorations of Buzz – or Andrew Campbell, as the court knew this presumably innocent man – Karen's wait was long. Each day she was all nerved-up to take the stand, but court business had never got that far.

When Buzz had been on the run for those six months, he was dealing from next-door-but-one to the police station. The last place they'd look. Karen was just as bold. She was staying at Gina's, though never going out. She was on edge there, but it was better than the isolation of a hotel. Besides, she knew the police would be round in seconds if there was any attempt to break in.

When DC Jones saw that it was going to be a couple of days still, and how frazzled his star witness was getting, he let Karen go back to London for a day and a night, helping escort her himself to the station.

As they left the Crown Court, a black car with four men in it was parked on double-yellows, right outside. She was surprised the police didn't move this car on, but just walked past it. Perhaps, she thought, these were plain-clothes officers too.

As they drove in a blue Astra, she noticed that they were going a very long way round. None of the officers in the car (two men, one woman) mentioned it. They had been over the same stretch of one-way system twice, clipping the same mini-roundabout in the same way, before Karen said, 'Blimey, we've gone half-way round the Reekin, here!' No-one said anything, and then she guessed. She looked back. The car was gone. When they pulled up at Piccadilly, she ran on to the train.

Four
DISCOVERY ─────────────────

I think Svetlana's got a new boyfriend. Another man, another lover. Oh no. I don't know if she's actually seeing him, but I've seen them together. Twice, now.

He drives a Land Rover Discovery. She got into the car with a quiet, sort of 'inward' smile. (No nuance of expression lasts for long in the possessive heart. Jealousy, that old caricaturist, is never far away. And what, pray, does that 'inward smile' tell us, Jealousy? What violence can you wreak on that? 'It's her not wanting to burst with joy at her luck at getting into the car with this man.' Thank you for that illumination, Jealousy.)

He corners the car gently. I think they're going to his. I don't know where he lives. I hope it's not far. My fingers hurt and I don't know how much longer I can hold on to the roof. I'm still winded from a pothole somewhere back there in a little one-way street in Soho. My numb fingers are frozen into position on the black graphite rim of the roof. If I fall off will they even notice?

He speeds up as we go past Warren Street station, heading north up into Camden. With my right ear on the roof, I can see the traffic of Marylebone underpass

coming up. For a second I see my own reflection in
the mirrored glass of Capital Radio Tower. Blimey, I
look like a madman.

Oh my god, the fucking bastard just ran a red light! I
felt like leaning over the front of the windscreen and
saying, 'Excuse me, it's not just your life at stake, you
know. You could've killed me then.'

Molten adrenalin and blood boiling through my
pumping temples assure me that my hands won't be
too numb for the ultraviolence to come. Oh yeah. He
may be this and this and that that I'm not, but he will
find that I am much, much, much and so much more
at home in the house of extreme violence than he. He
may have done boxing at his poshboy school, but no
matter. The greater the violence the more – alas – in
my element he will find me. And it _will get_ very violent. Oh, I can promise the cunt that. He will have a
new experience. A wholly new insight will enter his
dull brain, his dullard's soul. No doubt this brand new
level of experience will, consciously at least, be
washed away by time. Eventually all the surrounding
cliché of his convalescence, good friends taking him
wind-surfing when he's partially recovered, will do its
work, on one level at least. What mercy I show may
depend on what noises he makes or doesn't, and, I
suppose, on the tone of her remonstration as well:
what noises she makes or doesn't. Yes. Angry with
me, or loving and upset for him, stern and reproving
of me but not hateful, sensible of my pain, or hateful.
I really don't know which will be worse for me and
him, which tone of hers will cause me and him most
pain.

Enjoy your brief spell, son; enjoy your last gear changes, you monkey. Hell is coming. Which way I fly is hell; myself am hell. Why should I have all the hell – all locked up here with me? Why?

Now we're on narrower, smaller roads it doesn't hurt so much to hold on. I can even take one hand off the roof-rim every now and then and press it flat on the roof to balance that way. I don't press down too hard, even on fast swerves, because I don't want the metal to buckle noisily. His gear-changes are getting more fiddly and often now, the cornering more frequent and angular. (The art of being on the roof – for the nonce – is moving the hips quickly and silently, and nothing else.) Nearly home now. Time for action. Gratifyingly, now I come to plan and prepare what the next few minutes shall bring, I find that some subconscious part of my mind has everything all down pat. The scenario is worked out already. It is wonderfully clear, as only a few things ever are in life:

He parks and gets out of the car. He turns to point the car-alarm. I slide down in a leisurely way from the roof, stand up straight and say, 'Hello'. An initial element of surprise and moral shock which he won't recover from until he wakes up. I go up to him. He backs away. He knows I'll never stop. He knows I'm not sane at this point. I jump in the air and do a pedal kick. He falls for the dummy as if I've just invented the move, and parries the leg that pedals in the air a second, before the other leg kicks in. I catch him on the side of the jaw, and I bump into his chest with my other knee, landing on top of him. I'm first up. He stays down. It occurs

*to me, in the lucidity of my loud-beating heart, how much
the underside of the jaw resembles the toe of a man's shoe. It
is exactly like the representational toe on which a cobbler
slips a shoe before he works on it. Perhaps, then, if I catch
my toe flush and cobbler-perfect with the toe-shape of his
shine-a-buttercup underjaw, his head will come off his
stupid stump clean . . .*

This must be his street now then. A row of small terraces with green or blue or brown front doors right on
the pavement. He parks the car on the second attempt
(what a fucking wanker). The doors stay closed. Do
they know? They are both sitting in the car, headlights
still on. I can hear a hum of happy talk. They are enjoying the sweet spell of each other's company. It must
have been really difficult for them so close yet so far on
the long journey, only a handbrake and two seat belt
clicks away from the embrace which now they . . .

As my tears roll down the windshield, a spume of
chlorinaceous water comes up, followed by two windscreen wipes. Are they taking the piss? Are they
laughing at me? If they are then I will really get nasty –
but then I realise he just thinks that, on stopping, some
trickle of rainwater in the car's mini-guttering has
been jerked down, or that he must be under some still-
dripping deciduous tree, or something.

My frozen, numb fingertips mop my wet face like a
friendly stranger's cold touch, and in that instant I
know that only someone else's hands could carry this
through. The car doors open. What a time for that to
happen – just as my morale and my intent and fixity of

purpose and resolve has gone. Oh fuck – what am I gonna do now? What am I gonna do? I raise my head above what feels like a parapet. They stop outside his front door. He singles out his front-door key from a lumpy clutch of keys, and she interrupts him for a hug. (A fucking *hug* – not a kiss – how long has this been going on?) Averting my eyes from this disgusting embrace, I notice that the gold number on his tasteful green wooden door is an obscene 69.

I stand up on the roof, and step down noisily on to his bonnet. The lovers break off in time to see my giant's causeway stride stepping down from high bonnet to pavement: a triple-jump of descent, my lover. Maybe they can see I've been crying. Maybe they can't – in this dark street with its antique Victorian street-lamps (Mr Hyde, Jack the Ripper, brutal Billy Sykes).

Svetlana lets out a staccato cry of surprise – as if I could ever have hurt you, for fuck's sake. They back off.

'I see,' I say weightily, as if wronged, as if I was still going out with her.

What I *can* do – so that this hasn't been an entirely wasted trip, so that I don't pop into nothingness with sheer impotence – what I can do is now clear to me, seeing as they've retreated up the pavement a little, and I'm standing outside his front door. I punch my fist through the downstairs window. I kick in his front door; this takes quite a while and I'm worried Svetlana will start reasoning before I do it. Kick, kick, kick, jump and pedal-kick, and the wood around the lock splinters. Open Sesame. I step back to the edge of the pavement, pull out the metal inner from a green plastic bin and, with a bit of a run-up and a scream, throw it clean through an upstairs window (hopefully the bedroom). There, let cold winds come into their love nest just like they had into mine. I enjoy the spray of showering glass. One lethal dagger shard might have skewered my skull but hit the pavement between my scuffed shoes instead, and didn't break.

They are looking at me with a strange look of detached curiosity – frightened, yes, but puzzled too. This sets something nameless lurching in my stomach. What is it? He looks at his front door key, still singled-out between thumb and forefinger. He opens the door to number 63, and in they go.

Just don't talk to me for a while.

Five
THE STAND _____

There was a man whose hobby was to watch court cases from the public gallery. He was about sixty, with frizzy brown hair, thick sideburns and a brown checked jacket done up at the waist. He looked like Noddy Holder's dad. He came up to Karen in the corridor. 'It's been twelve years since someone last defended himself in a murder trial, hop. Oi been coming to court for twenty year, ooo, Oi never seen an atmosphere like this! Oi don't know if Oi can take it much longer, hep! Good luck, love, you'll do very well, you will.'

The witness who came out before her looked really ill. Trembling and drawn, a thin, sickly veil of perspiration covered her pale face.

Karen had made a decision whether to go in looking nice and smart and presentable, or whether to be herself. If she was going to be stressed out, she reasoned, she didn't want to feel uncomfortable as well.

She was led into the courtroom wearing denim hotpants over black tights. The denim shorts, which she had worn almost every day for two years, were covered all over in multi-coloured painted patterns: a pink flower on the rear pocket, lime green squiggles all over, a white star, a yellow smiley face, a heart and a cross in purple. She wore a baggy creamy-white linen top and a three-quarter-length black leather jacket.

Quite unexpectedly, the judge was absolutely beautiful. In her late forties, she had that type of face of an erstwhile screen goddess who now cares for animals – except with make-up on. Her blue eyes scanned the court without her moving her head. When she needed to look at a part of the court outside her field of vision, she turned her head in one clear movement and her panoptic eyes moved again. Occasionally, a stray strand of her platinum-blonde hair protruded from the white wig, as if she were Justice itself.

The bible's cold, shiny leather left Karen's palm. The prosecution rose.

'What is your name?'

'Karen Ann Doonan.'

'And where do you live?'

'I'm not going to answer that.'

'Why not?'

'I'm just not.'

The prosecution had never met her before, and had only read her statement. He was unprepared for this. 'Would you be prepared to write your address down so that it can be shown to the judge, so that we can proceed?'

'Yes.'

'When eventually I was called, I went in and ... you know when you get that feeling where you think, "I should be really scared, or I should feel something here," but it's not what you imagine. So then I felt quite calm to begin with.'

Karen sat on the floor of the boat as she recounted this. All hands were there, with the exception of Kevin, who kept to his little cabin in the prow as usual. 'The prosecution first runs through your evidence, and it's like doing a bloody exam, 'cos you read through your statement to begin with, and you wrote this two years ago, and you can't remember every last detail of what you wrote. He was asking me questions and being very nice and everything. And for that first hour you're getting all these look from the jury. And you're looking at them and they're looking at you, and you're thinking, "Oh shit, look at them, they're not gonna believe me. They're so straight, there's mommy with her specs on, these are the people who phone in to phone-ins." And also you get all these paranoias, you know. There's the black jurors bringing all their baggage with them. And there's all these really straight-looking older people . . .'

[MEMO TO SIDNEY LUMET – Below is a transcript of the trial. Could we, however, lose the following scene? I feel it adds nothing to the plot.]

REGINA VS ANDREW CAMPBELL

From the court transcript

THE CROWN CALLS WITNESS FOR THE
PROSECUTION ROBERT NEWMAN. HE
CANNOT BE FOUND FOR SOME TIME.
DETECTIVE CONSTABLE JONES LOCATES
WITNESS HIDING IN TOILET.

Q.C.: Are you Robert Newman of [. . .] Lane,
Camden, London? Are you Robert Newman of
[. . .] Lane, Camden, London?

MRS JUSTICE EVANS: Would you like a glass of
water?

(UNCLEAR TO WHOM FOLLOWING
REMARKS ARE ADDRESSED).

MR NEWMAN: 'All right, Kevin, Dean, Gary,
Jeggsy. Blimey, put that shooter away! How's the
Kung Fu going, Tony? Cor guvnor, bleedin' hell,
strike a light, Chris, Steve! Lads!'

WITNESS IS EXCUSED AND ASKED TO
STAND DOWN.

[I think you want some fast-paced scenes here
instead, Mr Lumet.]

Buzz had sacked his barrister five minutes into the

trial. He had been staring at Karen all through her evidence, but she hadn't met his gaze. This was the witness he had to destroy. Her statement included the following sentences: 'I would like to say that there was no way this incident was a fight between two men. It was just a straightforward aggressive attack by Buzz on the man who stood in front of me.'

Buzz stood up, flanked by two prison officers who were standing slightly behind him. He was free to pace about. He walked to the side, swayed, and then walked forward two paces.

REGINA VS ANDREW CAMPBELL

From the court transcript

THE ACCUSED CAMPBELL: Where do you live?

KAREN DOONAN: I've already said I'm not answering that question.

AC: But it's in Camden Town, London, though, isn't it?

KD: I'm not answering.

AC: You have a sister, don't you? She lives at 121 Horsham Road, Fallowfields, doesn't she?

KD: I'm not answering that. He's threatening me.

MRS JUSTICE SMITH: I'm going to recess the court for a few minutes.

(ADJOURNED FOR A SHORT WHILE)

_____

The jury filed out first, stepping through a narrow wooden door which, because sunk down a couple of steps, looked impossibly small. When the court was clear, the judge leaned forward.

Out in the corridor Karen was shaking.

The kindly fifty-year-old usher attended to her. 'Do you want a cigarette, love?' They brought her some fags and a cup of tea. She had one cigarette straight after the other.

'All right, take your time. When you're ready we can go back in.'

When Karen came back in the judge turned to her and gave her a warm smile that told her she was safe, that she was there to help her, that she was not alone.

Buzz's tactics were to confuse reality by pedantically repeating the written report of the events. Reality and the reported version never match entirely; a wedge may always be driven between the two. Karen felt like Buzz was asking a thousand tiny questions all going off in different directions, and that her sense of what had actually happened was shooting off hither and thither with them.

REGINA VS ANDREW CAMPBELL

From the court transcript

AC: And the man has not fallen yet?

KD: Well, not yet, no.

AC: Are you saying that you saw the head butt?

KD: Well, that is what I said in my statement, and that is what is true.

AC: You saw the head butt, but the man had not fallen, he was still standing?

KD: The thing is, you have asked me to read my statement, but you keep interrupting it; and you are not achieving anything because the next statement says that, you know, the next thing I saw was that the man fell to the floor.

AC: We just want you to read the statement. We are trying to establish at what time you did see him fall to the floor?

KD: But if you listen, then you will know, because it is the next thing I saw.

AC: Yes, but what I'm trying is to establish the incident itself in detail. What you are saying is that –

KD: I would have thought you'd have had a very clear memory of the incident.

MRS JUSTICE EVANS: Miss Doonan, let Mr Campbell ask you the questions as he wants and just answer them as they come, will you?

AC: Thank-you, ma'am. How long did you see the incident for?

KD: Those things happen in what appear to be slow motion, and, you know, I was so shocked because I really didn't think you would do something like that; I really didn't, and you know, the exact time length it took I don't know. It appears in my memory to be long and short at the same time. It is very confusing.

AC: The headbutting that you was observing.

KD: Well, I was observing – I observed the head butt and I observed what else is written in the statement.

AC: Just keep to what I'm saying.

KD: OK.

AC: Just keep to what I'm saying. Right. How tall was this person; can you remember, about?

KD: 'This person?'

AC: Who was standing in front of you . . . the victim?

KD: I remember him as being, I don't know, about – it's very hard – about five-foot-ten, and he was very slim, very slim build.

AC: And five-foot-ten?

KD: About that.

AC: Well, what?

KD: I can't be sure exactly; I wasn't actually looking precisely at the victim.

AC: Do you remember what he was wearing?

KD: I have no idea what the victim was wearing.

AC: So you cannot give a description of the victim at all?

KD: Not an accurate one, no.

AC: So you cannot give a description of the victim at all?

KD: I can give a vague idea of the person who I believed was stabbed, but to be quite honest –

AC: The person you believed –

MRS JUSTICE EVANS: Don't shout at the witness. Just allow her to finish.

KD: Well, I saw somebody on the floor after the incident and it is, as I said, two years ago, and I am doing my best to recollect everything, but I am not Karen Memory-Woman. My attention was mainly focused on the person we know as Buzz.

AC: OK, give a description of Buzz.

KD: Well, it's you.

AC: You're being cheeky now.

———————————————

Among both the Reds at Hogdale and the Arkness gangs, the word 'cheeky' had gravity. It was a formal word, a specific offence: 'cheeky' was what Glen had been.

———————————————

REGINA VS ANDREW CAMPBELL

From the court transcript

THE ACCUSED CAMPBELL: Who drove you home last night?

KAREN DOONAN: DC Jones drove me home last night.

AC: He drove you home *again* last night, you mean? Did you have a nice time, together, again, you and DC Jones?

KD: Yes, thank you, we had a very nice time. Myself, DC Jones and WPC Ridges. We went to Pizza Hut.

AC: OK. There is this part of your statement, page forty-seven, that I'm going to read to you. It says – you or the police you maybe owe favours to, wrote (this may not be your fault) – 'a commotion began and lots of people starting moving around . . .'

KD: Yes.

AC: 'As I am not very tall, *I couldn't really see much*. While people were moving around I got out of the way . . .'

KD: That's right, I moved a step backwards.

MRS JUSTICE EVANS: Just a moment. You read that in a misleading way, Mr Campbell.

AC: How did I read it in a misleading way, ma'am?

MRS JUSTICE EVANS: Because you paused as if there were a sentence: '. . . I couldn't really see very much.' New sentence: 'While people were moving around I got out of the way and moved.' That is not what it says and you know it; now read it.

AC: 'Once this occurred a general commotion began and lots of people started moving around. As I am not very tall, I couldn't really see very much while people were moving around. I got out of the way, and moved on to a raised step which moved me about five or six feet from the fight.'

KD: Yes.

AC: But you have just says, you have just says two contradicting things here. One is that you says earlier was that you was 'dragged out of the way', and here we have it now that you 'moved' out of the way.

KD: Well, it was 'moved', but I was actually –

AC: You says 'dragged'. There's a big difference.

KD: One of my friends moved me.

AC: She said 'dragged' earlier on today, ma'am. She said, 'somebody dragged me'.

KD: I did, I did actually say that.

AC: She did! She said, 'I was dragged', and now here it is in her statement that she 'moved'. So what was it? Was you moved or was you dragged?

KD: I was pulled out of the way by a friend of mine.

AC: So you're lying in this statement, then?

KD: No, in the main it is not incorrect, but that . . . I did actually move . . . but because . . . This is difficult to explain – because other people were not willing to give testimony, and I was not willing –

AC: We are not interested in other people not willing to give testimony. So you are saying that you move and walk away with people, and then when you look again you see a man falling? Is that correct?

KD: I'm sorry, can you run that past me again?

AC: What you have just said is that you have seen a man walk up and headbutt someone?

KD: Yes.

AC: Then you walk away six feet?

KD: Yes.

AC: Up a step?

KD: Yes.

AC: Then you look back and you see the man falling?

KD: The man was up against the fruit machines.

AC: No, we are not saying that; we are saying what you say, that is what you said.

(No reply)

MRS JUSTICE EVANS: Will you let her explain what she remembers; and will you stop barracking this witness?

AC: I am sorry.

KD: The incident as I can remember happened as in my statement. I must confess because of your aggressive manner and everything else I am now getting quite ... quite distressed, and, you know, wondering what I said last and what I am going to say now; and at the moment I don't think I am in a fit state to have to answer the question.

J: Do you want a few minutes?

AC: Yes. May I?

J: I will come back in at twenty-five past.

(ADJOURNED FOR A SHORT TIME)

AC: Are you okay?

KD: Thanks for the concern.

AC: I'm sorry.

J: Can we get on with the questions?

AC: Are you all right?

KD: I'm okay.

J: Just let us get on with the questions and get this cross-examination over.

———————

The main thrust of the defence was that it was not an attack, but a generalised scuffle. A fight had broken out between lots of people, and in that mêlée, who could say, beyond a reasonable doubt, which of all these people had stabbed 'this person' Glen? It being inadmissable in court that the accused Campbell was a convicted drug dealer, and there being no other apparent relation to this other man, what possible motive could there be either?

The simplest tasks seem the most unwieldly when someone is standing over you watching your every move critically. And this is what talking became. So many answers seemed to be slipping from her all wrong. She was in that nightmare where intention and execution won't match.

REGINA VS ANDREW CAMPBELL

From the court transcript

AC: In your statement you do not mention the word 'stab'. You do not even mention seeing anyone being stabbed. And yet in this dock you distinctly say you seen Buzz stab this man.

KD: I tell you why I can say that for certain. It is because of the actual train of events as they occurred. If you see a car going towards something, and it smashes into a wall, and then you see a dead cat underneath it, you know, without having seen the cat before, that the person has run over the cat, because now it's dead.

AC: So you are presuming, then, that is so?

KD: No, I'm not presuming, because the person on the floor was there and he was stabbed.

AC: But you says you did not see it in this statement. You have not mentioned anyone being stabbed in your statement.

KD: I saw an arm go back with a knife and –

AC: Oh, I see. You saw an arm go back.

(No reply)

MRS JUSTICE EVANS: Just allow the witness to finish what she wants to say. You wanted to explain what you saw.

KD: And the next thing the man is on the floor injured.

AC: So you did not actually see a stab?

KD: I saw somebody putting an arm forward with a knife. I did not see the exact moment of penetration into somebody's flesh.

AC: So why did you say you had seen a stab?

KD: Because the person was lying on the floor, and had obviously been stabbed, and the only person near him was you, and you obviously stabbed him.

AC: But you said . . . you came in here when the prosecution was questioning you and you says, 'Buzz walked up and stabbed him,' and now you are saying that you just seen his hand go forward. You said there are people milling around obscuring your view, so why did you say you had seen a stab, you don't know what could have happened because you couldn't see!

KD: For a second I couldn't see; yes, it's possible that in that second anything could've happened. In that second or two seconds, you know, aliens could have landed in little silver spaceships, but we know that didn't happen, did it?

AC: Did you see the knife enter any part of the body?

KD: No.

AC: So you did not see a stab, then.

KD: Yes I did, yes I did . . . I did.

MRS JUSTICE EVANS: Will you just pause a moment while I make a note, please? Is this right: you saw Buzz with a knife in his hand?

KD: Um-hmm.

JUDGE: You saw his arm move towards the victim?

KD: Yes.

JUDGE: You then saw the victim bleeding?

KD: I saw *afterwards* the victim was bleeding.

JUDGE: And you *deduced* that the victim . . . ?

KD: Yes, I think it is reasonable to assume.

AC: She presumed, ma'am, she presumed!

JUDGE: You put it to her that it is a presumption.

AC: Is that a presumption?

KD: I think it is more than reasonable to presume.

JUDGE: You say: 'I think it is a reasonable presumption,' but you accept it is a presumption because you did not see the knife entering the body?

KD: Well, I can't say that in the normal sense of the word, you know, I can't, I can't . . . be . . .

JUDGE: It's all right. I just want to clarify.

KD: You know, it's a presumption – but these are just words and barriers. From all my past experiences of life I would say it was a stabbing.

AC: But you didn't see it enter the body, did you? Yes or no?

KD: I think this is quite pedantic.

AC: Oh, do you really?

KD: Yes, I do.

AC: Just give me a straight answer now. Did you see the knife enter the body?

KD: This is just a case of reiteration.

AC: It is not a case of reiteration, it is a case of getting the facts.

KD: No, it is just boring repetition.

AC: I'll remember that. Did you see the knife enter the body?

KD: I did not actually see penetration.

AC: Thank you, that is what we are after. And you did not see a stabbing then?

KD: Actually, you know, I'm not the one that's accused of anything here, and I would quite like it if you treated me a bit more civilly.

AC: Well, just speak what you saw.

KD: If you were to be a bit more reasonable, perhaps, you know, I would not be up here trembling and being a nervous wreck, and this would all be a lot better for you. I'm sure it's not helping you any to be perceived as being aggressive.

AC: I'm not being aggressive.

JUDGE: Mr Campbell, what the witness says is not unreasonable. You should not intimidate her. I know that you're –

AC: Ma'am I –

JUDGE: Will you allow me to finish my sentence? You know that you are being allowed a good deal of latitude in your manner of questioning because you are unrepresented, and I ask you not to abuse the privileges that you are being given. Now then, will you please treat the witness more civilly, and, in particular, allow time for the witness to answer?

AC: You did not see the knife enter the body, right?

KD: I did not see penetration of the blade into a body.

AC: And so you were lying again!

Six
ON A CLEAR DAY _____

That New Year's Eve, me and the fugitive Karen both had nowhere to go. I'd spent Christmas alone and sent Svetlana (who was in Moscow) a message via the Ukrainian or Cossack Hotel receptionist: 'I miss you, love Kev.' The message she'd got, written in his peasant hand, transcribed from broken English and the whistling of long-distance undersea phone-cables, was the romantic, 'Mr Miss You called from Kiev.'

Why didn't I drop Karen off at hers after the party? Going to mine for a coffee (at three a.m.) became her staying over on the couch, became her sharing the bed, but just for comfort's sake. By then I was on to Lust's Sensory Accumulator whereby you say to yourself, 'All I need is to see that one shirt button unfastened, and that'll do me. That's all I need. Then I'll be able to go back to being normal. That single shirt button is the be-all and end-all, the whole universe is snagged on it, nothing else has ever been so important. I just need to see just that undone, that's all.' Only . . . once the shirt button is undone, you can then see the semi-transparent black lacework of the Wonderbra. And Lust's Sensory Accumulator kicks in again . . . now all

I need now is . . . now all I need now is . . . and now all I need now is a new soul.

Sex with Karen that New Year's Eve had the sensationalism of roof-ledges or desecration, but there was an ugliness there too, a cowardly equivocation. Because I didn't want to admit responsibility for what I was doing, I was – um – masochistically struggling. (Ask Tammy or Dolly here, Ken. Sorry to get weird here, pal.) Karen had to scratch her 'recalcitrant' one, hard and deep with long nails. As stupid as a man with a hard-on, did I think I was doing my penance and sin at the same time, as she dug her long nails in? Truly, 'a man makes a woman the cross he crucifies himself on', as Lawrence says.

Each day of the New Year I check the scars and weals in the bathroom mirror. What have I done? Only four days before she returns. Three and a half days. Three days. Had they gone down? If I look at them less will they vanish quicker? Three and a half days . . .

I hesitate to say it, but maybe one good thing has come out of this. I don't know whether it's to do with having been in love or whatever, but I think I'm weaned off of casual sex. I slept with Merry the other night. (She'd just split up from her boyfriend. We were in the same boat.) Sleeping with Merry simply reminded me that it wasn't Svetlana's body I was holding. Don't get me wrong, I wasn't, while sleeping with Merry, trying to pretend that I was with my tall Svetlana or anything like that: I wasn't trying to lay her ghost. No, it's just

165

that while me and Merry were – you know – I was just reminded that it wasn't her. If this was Svetlana, I was thinking, the small of her back would be here, she would be holding me a little higher, a little lower, the noises would be different, the breasts would be there, she would be failing to do something I wanted her to do here, and there would be a feeling of emptiness and not-being-loved round about now.

Like a controlled experiment to demonstrate Svetlana's irreplaceability, Merry is – guess what? – physically perfect. Objectively speaking, her bod is the best bod I've ever seen, and yet she couldn't hold a candle to Svetlana. There just wasn't that ole spark, that awe, that fear, love and magic – no matter what I did with her. (Lord knows I tried, Kenny. Heroically, valiantly, I tried. You know, Kenny, I bent her over, slapped her around, I got her to dress up, let me film her, had her strip and do a sexy dance. Ho-hum. It all seemed to be happening at one remove, under a blanket of sensory numbness.)

I kept looking down and seeing it wasn't her. I was more lonely than ever.

It's ironic, Kenster; because when me and Svetlana first started going out I felt sexless. She stayed over several times before we even slept together. And when we did have sex I was self-conscious. A real woman for once, and not a fetishised abstraction, perhaps. Someone who knew people I knew. I could get it up and that, but I used to have to stop.

I remember watching *Roman Holiday* at this time. Did my odd lack of lust simply mean that I'd been elevated into a kind of Gregory Peck and Audrey

Hepburn existence? That would be the best news, I thought. They dance cheek-to-cheek to sentimental airs of love and morality. He never, even after she sleeps over at his, tries to get fingers and tops. Gregory's pecker is a sleeping giant, somewhere deep within those baggy-crotch trousers of the time. He's cerebral and self-possessed, but no doubt a tiger when the time is right.

Or did my libidinous changedown mean something else? Was I in a terrible TV play, all bedroom recrimination and ugliness? No, I said to myself, it's just I've never loved the whole woman before. It's ironic, Kenny, I'm saying, that that body had now become the Platonic Ideal. The full-colour 3-D illustration in the _Encyclopaedia of my Loins_ under 'Woman's Body' [See also 'Rejection', 'London', 'Night', 'Day', 'Roaring Traffic's Boom', 'Lonely Room (silence of)' . . .].

Hope seeks refugee status in lust, however. Drove a couple I'd met at a party back to their flat which was on the way home. Brazilian and flirty, the woman kept exhorting me to come up for a hot chocolate. I knew this was because she knew I was holding (she'd seen me buy a kotchel of E at the party). Hope, however, said, 'Maybe – just maybe – her stiff-backed, rather formal boyfriend will take me to one side, while she's making the hot chocolate, and say, 'I wonder if you could do me a favour, old man? Since a motorbike accident in Rangoon, I have been unable to satisfy my wife's – shall we say – _needs_. Once every five years we select a suitable man. But I warn you, that's five years of pent-up sexual energy. I cannot promise you that she won't grab your hair and call you a slut; I can't vouch-safe that she won't be satisfied until you have done every abomination under the sun ..."' etc. etc.

There were no parking spaces and I dropped them off in the next street.

I hesitate to say I'm weaned off of casual sex, because of what happened with Tina.

Tina was in foster care with me. We met over a decade ago, when I was sixteen and she was eleven. My last year, her first. I've always been like an older brother to her. When she got to sixteen I thought, 'will I shag her?' But, even during my sluttish years, I never did, and this became one of the things I liked best about myself. Of all the men she knew, I thought, this was a purer thing. She lived in Manchester, and I felt like this kindly, neutral bookish professor with his charming daughter. I liked that role. She'd even stayed with me a couple of times, and, despite me seeing her in a white bath towel on the landing (having hung around for some time on various landing pretexts), the resolve had stayed.

She came round a week or so after Svetlana ended with me: to Crag Misogylvania, over whose chimneys the forked lightning spelt 'R-E-V-E-N-G-E'.

Now that car-theft wasn't enough she was doing some GCSEs at the age of twenty-two, and I helped her with 'To What Extent is Grief and Loss a Theme in *Hamlet*?'. She was down with a girlfriend and they were staying at a B&B somewhere. Tina came over on her own, while her friend tried to track down her father at Somerset House. Even though nothing happened, this was the only time I never loved her when I was with her (the only time in ten years). I didn't love her because I couldn't see her; all I had were the cold eyes of lust. I saw her consciousness as an obstacle, something to be manipulated or dodged. I was engineering situations, contriving scenes. To my shame I almost made a pass. Almost . . . ?

Just as she was leaving, I asked for a hug. She had a shorty jumper on with a bit of inner-city-pale midriff showing. My 'hugging' hands were on the cold vertebrae of her backflesh.

'Is that a bra?' I enquired matter-of-factly, as if researching for a Government white paper on Bras Worn by Young Women since the General Election.

'No,' she said, smiling a tad awkwardly, embarrassedly, 'it's a vest.'

'Oh you mean one of those mini-top things?' I asked, smiling, because I was just fooling, of course. Of course.

She nodded with the same uneasy smile, and I lifted up her jumper to look. (SHAME. SHAME. SHAME.)

For the record it was a black mini-top, and there was a surprising amount of breastage happening. Pale and, as they say, full.

Shortly before she left, I'd been talking about Svetlana (I was talking about Svetlana universally, and it was more a case of people coming within earshot, really). I mentioned that I'd chucked her once, and said this with no more reflection than a kind of amazement or head-shaking disbelief. And _she_ said, Tina said: 'Ah, rejection – the old male ego. It's because she chucked you this time that you're upset.'

Bitterly I reflected that a little learning is a terrible

thing. Where the fuck, I thought, had *she* got the phrase 'old male ego' from? That's a sign that I should sever all remaining links with the underclass. They don't have any nuance. We can't be friends now that I'm older and more sophisticated, because she's always going to hurt me by blurting out some half-arsed piece of blithe second-hand crassness. Only trouble is, she was completely right. She'd hit the nail on the head. (That's because she was still the bright girl I'd always loved, even if there was no love in me to see it anymore.) Bang on, Tina. Not only did I love everything but the girl with Svetlana, now I miss everything but the girl, too. Loss has a habit of becoming all loss. (Put that in your Silvine exercise-book, Tina.) I don't love anyone; I don't miss anyone. This pain is all mine.

I chucked *Svetlana* once. And I never felt more in the real world (never more like her). That night – for the only time in my life – I *thought*. I was happily rational.

You know I'm always yearning for the Big Epiphany, and that night – for once – I had one. That said, my Big Epiphany was the type of realisation everyone else knew anyway. It's like: 'And for the first time I suddenly realised that some shops are open on Sunday.'

However . . .

I was up on the roof-ledge about an hour after I'd thrown her out of the house. Strangely calm and complete, I looked at four lanes of traffic, the old cemetery and the innumerable rooftops and impenetrable windows . . . and for once I felt part of it all, connected to the big hubbub.

I stared down at the cemetery and the sight felt rich, rewarding, physically so, in the actual eyes. The very eyeball itself felt good. I became the most recent person on earth to see that everyone in every single or double plot had known life in all its extremes. They had all known extreme pain and stress; all been overjoyed. All had been enchanted; and they'd all known extreme grief so bad they thought it must be meant for another species.

In the past, when I looked at the grave of – I don't know – *Amos Griffiths – Died 1876*, I hadn't seen it. I just thought he'd kind of worked in the fields, (never breaking into a sweat) had come home, had a bit of beer and bread on a wooden table authentic to the period. One day he had stretched out for a kip in the utilitarian-no-sex bed (wearing a white nightcap) and died. A vicar with a wide-brimmed hat and Englebert Humperdink sideburns had done the business. The lichen-covered headstone – popular at the time – had been put in place. The same thing with *Eliza Good-bodycoate – d. 1802*. 'Och isn't the price of calico dear a bit oh I'm dead.' I never saw them as what George Eliot (their contemporary) calls 'equivalent centres of self'. (Otherwise I'd never have been able to dig 'em up and fuck 'em! Don't worry, I'm only joking Kenny! *It's a .44 and I know how to get it through customs.* Hahahaha!!)

And all those people in cars flowing up on to the flyover – red lights going away, white lights coming forward. All . . . all had experienced extreme feelings and thoughts, the keen edge of life, some time or other – in between The Steve Wright Breakfast Show and the funfair where they won the rear-window Garfield.

171

Oh, and out there on the roof the wind tousled my hair like a welcome home, of course. But suddenly I didn't want the cinematic or the transcendent. My only fear out there on the roof-ledge at that moment was this: that the weight of negative habit would come to bear and obliterate this new-found rational human. Like the heart-attack that does for the penitent suicide after his successful stomach-pump. That was my fear: that I might go back to being the man I was before I met her, head stuffed with rubbish. Oh Lord, please don't let me be back-sliding.

Seven
SVETLANA _____

Svetlana. The name was never shortened. She was Svetlana, plain *Svetlana*, in the morning, standing six-feet-two in muddy trainers at the foot of the bed, her hands wet with dew, pulling the duvet off this grumpy sleepyhead. She was Svetlana in slacks. She was Svetlana on the dotted line. She was Svetlana dancing at the Romanian Embassy with some grinning fucking diplomat, and in my possessive arms for the next dance she was still, alas, only ever Svetlana. But what could I do?

'I do not like eet when you call me "Svezzer", Kevin.'

Jealousy was a big, dirty player in the argument that led to me chucking her that day, but not the start. The argument started about walking.

She took walking seriously. We'd visited Billy Hurley, and gone for a walk around Exmoor. She had map, routes, a time to set off, a time to get back. She had her own wellies too. A bit like riding boots, I'm pleased to report. I found some right-sized green gumboot wellies in the lobby of the hotel and put them on.

If you happen to see the most beautiful girl in the world, she'll be walking very fast. She liked to charge along. The different speeds we walked at became a big issue. I liked to saunter and ruminate and reflect. For her it was like orienteering. We were always in perfect step, but she was fast and I was slow.

Now, you would've thought that here was an argument made to be won. Wasn't the whole weight of Western art and literature on my side? If this was *Planes, Trains and Automobiles*, for just one example, then she was the Steve Martin character (timetable-ridden materialist) in need of benign derailing by John Candy (yours truly, with a pain in my heart that'll kill me).

'Life isn't like a feelm!' she cried.

I never did anything with my day because I knew from an early age that all activity was mere 'activity'. She was always charging around, cramming a hundred things into each day, for exactly the same reason.

A little later in the row she said, 'You don't love me.' She said, 'You're in love with an idea of me.'

'What do you mean? I *love* you. I love *you*. You know, I think about you all the time. I . . . I have conversations with you when you're not there.'

'That's eet! *When I'm not there*. Eet's all in your head!'

I saw her as life personified, and I kind of hoped it would rub off. Like, when she goes to a city, Kenny – Prague, Barcelona, Moscow – it opens up. To me it's dead walls and a diner. To her, well, she knew people there, she knew the places to go. When you were with her, you'd be kind of on the inside of the city like life itself. Whereas I dwelt in regions of dull abstraction, she loved oysters, knew wines, champagnes, loved motorbikes, Camel Lights, clothes, sleep, knew all the smiling restauranteurs – (always a bit *too* fucking pleased to see her, if you ask the frowning escort). She dressed in brown and loved this terra-firma. Like life she had no time for the past, and there was often something pitiless about her. Like life she was insistently political, hated the grand poetic half-truth and allowed no shirking. 'But what do you *really* think?' she'd ask. She was adult and a realist and I was childish and a fantasist. (I'm sure if you showed this part of the letter to Dolly or Tammy, they'd just say, 'In other words she was a wooman and he was a maan'!)

Within seconds of us splitting up that first time, however, I was able to see her as her for once. With almost an outsider's concern, I felt sorry for her as she carried her things down the three flights of stairs. The pathos of seeing her walk down the stairs, suddenly a child again with the menfolk being nasty. An institutional, locked room, a foreign man in an army uniform shouting at my poor baby about the undesirability of her parents.

She phoned next day, a Sunday. 'I left my earrings there.' After my night of elevated contemplation on the balcony, I was Mr Magnanimity (North London Region).

'I'll bring them round.'

'Are you sure?'

'Yeah.'

I was keen to surprise her with the new-deal me. I felt warm towards the world. Perhaps she had expected me to snarl and snap and slam down the phone. She sounded surprised. That was a new tone of voice I hadn't heard in her before, too.

She answered the door and gave me a thick, warm kiss. I'd never seen formal Svetlana dressed so casual. She had on raggedy jeans and a jersey of softest bjorkest wool. Her hair was up in a French plait. (Jesus, *sorry*, Kenny. Of course a gruff, regular guy like you wouldn't know a fag thing like that. Forgive me. Her hair was just up, OK? Like, you know, up.)

There was a twinkle in her eye, and I thought how much I *liked* her. Agape ruled, and things were more perfect between us than ever. Things were exactly how I hoped they would be between us when I first met her. I had the same feeling of courtliness and polite regard, as when she first helped us both to some champagne in an ante-room away from the others at a reception for students and their friends at the language school. I felt privileged, caught up in a better, more graceful world, just through a grace in her being. (Things were different a week after bringing the earrings round. The way she nagged when I opened the back-door to wander around her little garden, and sneered when I put honeycomb in my tea and it didn't dissolve like she'd told me it wouldn't.)

Round at her house that Sunday, I wondered whether this accord meant we were meant to be friends, or whether it was a new beginning. She sat in front of me and did a bit of yoga. I arranged to meet her in a Japanese restaurant.

Before she walked in I knew it was her, and looked up to see a middle-aged man with a bald head and a grey suit.

Before she walked in I knew it was her, and saw a mother and daughter in two generations of specs.

Before she walked in I knew it was her – and there she was. Black jeans over her high thighs. Will she ever see me? Perhaps she'll go out again and I'll have to explain that I was there, only invisible through sheer nerves, and too shy to shout out.

'Hello.'

'Hello.'

The feeling of seeing her as her, however, was still there. Before, she had been my sun, my moon, my stars, but I never let her finish a sentence. And now – well whaddyaknow – it turned out she was quite a girl.

Now we were so very far away from those frail mortals who *argued*; now we *differed*, and were curious about each other's workings.

She was talking about being nearly thirty-two, and that it was possible that she'd already lived the majority of her life.

'I'm surprised you're frightened of death,' I said. 'I always had this theory that – ' She raised her eyes to the fretted wooden ceiling at the word 'theory'. I grinned.

'No, go on,' she said, leaving an eyebrow raised throughout the following.

'Oh, only that those who have had easy lives are frightened of death, and the rest of us see it as a sleep, as a "who can say he is really happy until he is dead" type of thing. I think you're either frightened of death or of pain.'

'Oh, I don't like pain either.' She re-filled my saki thimble. (I must have been too restrained and formal even for her.) 'I just theenk I don't want to miss everything that's happening. I can't imagine the worl' without me.'

'Isn't that just egotism, though?'

'No, it's not, it's the opposite. Eet's the thought of all these people going around and liffing lifes, all this will be going on, you know, everythink – and I won't be a part of eet.'

'That's how I feel now!'

'No, but how do you really feel?' In the same way that she would always counter the grand, poetic half-truth or theory with levity, she would not let flippancy go by without gravity. 'Come on, you don't feel like that.'

'No, I do, as it goes,' I said, though worried that the truth would make me unattractive to her.

Epiphanies don't take. That's because – let the dying man use the first person plural – we don't have habits of thought which allow us to reflect on our own experience; instead, we have habits of leisure to purge ourselves of experience. People no longer have a defined view of the world. There have been so many radical discoveries in the last seventy years, we think, 'What's the point?' If we nail our colours to any mast, it will inevitably be shown to be wrong. We think there's a wisdom in the hedged bet, the floating vote, the non-denominational. Without structures, the internal life becomes so amorphous as to be negligible.

After the meal, me and Svetlana stood on my balcony. My arms were at first tingling and then aching with the not-touching of her. I felt incomplete until my arms were round her, like a phantom limb, a phantom girlfriend. We looked out at the city. To me, by then, it was just buildings again. Early evening lights coming on before the sun's gone down. It looked like a model of London, as if there were a sheet of glass as thick as the foreground between me and the cityscape. To me, it looked like an undertaking, one you'd enter into at your peril. If you were lucky, you'd come out not damaged, not physically anyway, but perhaps messed up emotionally. It looked friendly and twinkling as a sentimental concept but not as a thing. As a thing, an actual entity, it was hard concrete and danger.

Svetlana – and I asked her so I know – she saw where her friends were and imagined what it was like at ground level there. She traced the out-of-sight streets. She wondered how area subtly shifts ambience, and at what point somewhere good became somewhere horrible and then somewhere good again. She mentally nipped through the invisible side streets and back-doubles in a car, far away.

Two tones.

'It's beautiful, isn't it?' I mumbled, thinking I'd lost my sense of wonder, of genuine rapport with things.

'Yes. Beautiful,' she said. And it was somehow a sign of her greater love for life and London that _she_ was the first to turn away and go back inside. I hung about outside, meanwhile, waiting for the stasis to break or something to happen on the dead skyline.

Eight
SECRET AFFAIR _____

Karen was totally alone. The only person who could have any idea what it was like, it occurred to her, was him. He too was at bay, alone, fighting for his life, stressed-out and fearful. Only the two of them in this whole expanse of building had their whole futures at stake, their very lives.

The judge was to clear the court twelve times in all, due to Buzz intimidating witnesses. During Karen's evidence alone, she had cleared the court six times. Round Seven.

_____

REGINA VS ANDREW CAMPBELL

From the court transcript

THE ACCUSED CAMPBELL: Then you went home, and did you speak about it when you arrived home?

KAREN DOONAN: I lived by myself.

AC: Then you went home by yourself?

KD: I did.

AC: Did you like this person Buzz?

KD: Well, he did not seem like the sort of person that would . . . I had occasion to think he was all right, you know.

AC: Did you speak to him often?

KD: I spoke to him several times, yes.

AC: Did you speak to him in pubs?

KD: Usually outside pubs, but once in a nightclub called Strut.

AC: Where is that?

KD: That's on Jermyn Street, isn't it?

AC: So you saw him often?

KD: I saw him several times, yes. He was always around Wythenshawe.

AC: Did you share any funny times with him?

KD: Not, really, no.

MRS JUSTICE EVANS: Did you say 'funny times'?

AC: Funny times, amusing times.

KD: Just sort of chit-chat and mildly entertaining conversation.

AC: You said yesterday that you have a friend called Louise?

KD: I did not say yesterday I had a friend called Louise, did I?

AC: Don't get lippy! Just answer the questions. Have you got a friend called Louise?

KD: Yes, I have.

AC: Does she know Buzz?

KD: She does, indeed, but I am surprised you want to bring up Louise.

MRS JUSTICE EVANS: Don't you ask questions, Miss Doonan. Carry on.

AC: Have you and Louise ever fallen out?

KD: We certainly have. Excuse me, I would like to talk to somebody about something that is happening at the moment, and I don't know what to do about it. Can I talk to somebody before the questioning continues?

MRS JUSTICE EVANS: That really is very difficult. Are you feeling intimidated in some way?

KD: I am actually feeling a bit edgy about some of the questions being asked.

MRS JUSTICE EVANS: Yes, I am afraid I must ask you to carry on answering questions. If I think there is anything improper in the questions I shall stop them, but at the moment I feel that they should be asked and answered.

KD: Okay, righty-ho.

———————————

Karen had fallen out with Louise because Louise, claiming to be thinking of Karen, but perhaps only thinking of herself, had told the police that Karen was in hiding because a contract had been out on her: in effect, that Karen wasn't going to testify. But the reason Karen felt edgy was something else.

Louise was too drunk to drive one night, and needed to go home to get some more cash and to change, because the people she was with were going out clubbing. Buzz offered to drive her home, back to her mum's. Once there, she ran in, came out again, and they started driving back to the pub. She noticed that they weren't going the right way, and asked, 'Where are you going?'

'Oh, it's a short-cut.'

Then later, 'Look, where are you going?'

'I've got to pop in and see someone first. It won't take long.'

The roads had less and less street-lights, and were more and more deserted and out of the way. The sleeping aluminium hangars of the industrial estate went by (Multilever, Invicta), so did cul-de-sacs of the self-styled enterprise zone. They drove along blond asphalt with a thin strip of tarmac running across the road every three or four heartbeats.

'Take me back to the Cottage!'

He said nothing. She had managed to get the seat-belt off without him noticing, and with the mini doing about forty, she opened the passenger door and rolled out of the car.

She went to the police next day, having made her way home with only minor cuts that night, but what could they do? He hadn't actually *done* anything. This experience with Buzz was one reason Louise panicked and phoned the police when Karen had told her not to.

———————

REGINA VS ANDREW CAMPBELL

From the court transcript

MRS JUSTICE EVANS: Will you continue, Mr Campbell?

AC: So you and Louise have fallen out?

KD: We have.

AC: How long have you been friends?

KD: We are actually friends again now, but we did fall out. But we have been friends about two to three years.

AC: Were you friends when you met this Buzz?

KD: Yes, we were good friends.

AC: Did you have a clandestine affair with Buzz?

KD: I beg your pardon? Did I? No. I can't believe it.

AC: Did you have a secret affair with Buzz?

KD: No, absolutely definitely not.

AC: So you did not sleep with Buzz?

KD: I think we take it that 'no, absolutely definitely not' means not, definitely not.

AC: While you was seeing him round the Wythenshawe area, did you have a boyfriend?

KD: Yes, I did. I had two, actually.

AC: Two boyfriends?

KD: Yes.

MRS JUSTICE EVANS: I hope this cross-examination is to some purpose, Mr Campbell, and not simply designed to embarrass the witness?

AC: No, ma'am, it is not designed to embarrass, I am trying to explore.

J: I hope you will get to the point of it soon.

AC: I put it to you that you did have an affair with Buzz.

KD: I can't believe you're doing this.

AC: And I put it to you that you did sleep with him.

KD: Well, my reply would be that I would certainly have known your name beforehand if I was having an affair with you.

AC: That is precisely it. You are saying that you have spoken to a person on numerous occasions, seen him about, and the only time – you have already admitted yourself – the only time you supposedly found out his name was after the incident?

KD: That is absolutely true, but there's no need to shout.

_____

In her statement, Karen had said that she 'didn't know him as Buzz until after the incident', meaning that she didn't know Andrew Campbell was Buzz's real name until after the incident.

_____

REGINA VS ANDREW CAMPBELL

From the court transcript

AC: But you have spoken to him? You even admitted that he asked you out?

KD: That is right, he did.

AC: And if a person talks to you and says: 'Will you go out with me?' Blah, blah, this, surely you would want to employ their name before you even spoke to them? It's not as if you spoke to him once or twice, but, you say, numerous occasions?

KD: Not wishing to sound immodest, but people quite often ask me out. Very strange people ask me out, and I have no wish to find out their name and whatever they do. I have no desire to go out with them at all, and you are one of those people. I had absolutely no desire to go out with you whatsoever, and the reason I did not want to know your name was that I thought there was something a bit peculiar about you, and I wanted to distance myself.

AC: That can't be done. How did this Buzz ask you out?

KD: Well, like, you said if I got two A's in my A levels, then you'd take me out . . . needless to say, I failed.

———————————

A sudden, deep silence kinked the intense, ugly atmosphere. Then, unimaginable a moment ago, everyone in the whole courtroom (except Buzz and the judge) burst out laughing.

Karen was suddenly aware of how high up the witness box actually made her. Until then, she had felt trapped and penned there while he roamed and paced below. Now she felt like she was looking down on him from a great height and a great distance.

Her eyes were buoyant and glinting as they met his. He looked away and looked back again. To his irritation, her beaming expression was *exactly* as he'd left it, even though the whole courtroom laughter had now stopped. It was as if she were marvelling at something new she was seeing as she looked at him. He turned a page of his notes, then raised his head. As his menacing dead stare met her gaze, however, he suddenly had to examine something in her full-beam eyes, and his look changed to scrutiny. In that glance something passed between Karen and Buzz. They both, at exactly the same moment and with equal amazement, realized who was the strongest.

Nine
THE KNIFE _____

Buzz had a plan to escape from the courthouse.

'You couldn't possibly have seen the colour of the knife,' he shouted. 'You're going on hearsay!'

'No, I know what colour the knife was.'

He made Karen read out her statement where she said that it reminded her of a Swiss Army type knife.

'How did you *know* it was a Swiss Army knife?' he hollered.

'I didn't. In my statement I clearly put it *reminded* me of a Swiss Army type knife. I'm not a knife expert; that's just what it reminded me of.'

'I want to demonstrate that there's no way she could have seen me with that knife. Can you pass me the knife?'

Karen stood there, thinking, 'she's never going to allow this,' just waiting for the judge to say no. Nothing was said. The knife was being passed to him.

'*No!*' cried Karen. 'No, no, no, no, no, no.' She started to back out of the witness box. 'No, I don't care. I don't care, you can put me in prison for contempt of court. I'm not staying in here with him, with that knife. *No!* You can do what you like; no, no, no, no.'

The judge spoke calmly to the usher who had the knife and was just about to hand it to Buzz. 'I don't think that's a very good idea; perhaps the prosecution can help here. If you would hold the knife as directed by the defence? Thank you.'

The *Nellie* makes her way through the dark night. As she slips quietly between Woolwich and Rotherhithe, the tiny lights of her windows are the only warm-looking things visible. The boat passes black outlines of industrial buildings, chimneys and an Esso storage tank as big as a house. Light from the river reflects up, catching the aluminium material covering some exterior lagging.

Outside in the night, a hundred yards from the boat, on the chill surface of the river, the wind flicks over the hard, tightly-rucked water, making some of the extraordinary noises the unattended world makes.

'And I had to hold the knife as well demonstrate,' said Karen over the subdued murmur of the boat's engine. 'I thought that was really sick. I had to hold the knife to demonstrate how I would have been able to see the colour of the handle. There's something horrible about – I mean, when I was holding it I didn't feel comfortable. I dunno, you imagine the dead person's spirit somehow intertwines with this object. You don't want to be disrespectful to it, you know what I mean? This is the item that killed him. Do you understand what I'm saying? I just didn't like it. I didn't feel comfortable at all. I said, "I don't wanna do it," and they said, "Well, you have to, to demonstrate the angle and how it happened," and I just thought, "this is so unnecessary."'

She had a swig of wine and lit up another fag. We were all silent. When she spoke again there was a tone of distress in her soft, husky Leeds drawl.

'And then they wanted to see how it was done, and when I was doing it there was no way I could give it that force; I thought there was something really vulgar in doing that. It just didn't seem right.'

She held the knife above the panel of the witness-box, and did one and then two half-hearted and slow upper-cuts with her head averted from the knife. This scene presented itself badly to the jury. It looked like that moment when a convincing liar is put on the spot by being asked to extemporise from an angle they haven't covered, and you can see the wind leave the sails of the lie. The Crown Prosecutor who, on the whole, felt himself lucky with the calibre of witnesses, and in particular this, his star witness, had a moment of intense disappointment. Karen, however, felt only relief when the knife was taken out of her right hand, and she could go back merely to being shouted at. Clear and composed, she looked straight ahead, having acquitted herself somewhere else. She winced one more time, though, when out of the corner of her eye she saw the usher put the open red knife into the thick polythene exhibit bag.

Ten
REMEMBRANCE DAY ⸻

By this time, we had sailed through Greenwich Light-Vessel Automatic and out into the Wash. Everyone on board the *Nellie* was turning in for the night; hooking their hammocks, or laying out their sleeping bags. While they slept, the Captain would run the boat up through German Bite. Gina was to pick Karen up when we put in near Hull next morning. From there, the two sisters would drive back across the Pennines for the verdict, which was now only a few days away.

I stayed up a little longer, talking to Claud who was a friend of Polish Joe's. They were the two oldest on the boat, and the two foreigners. Small and Greek, Claud was working on a singular project: part quantum mechanics, part cartography, part theology. He was drawing a map of the spiritual world.

'Everything has its physics, its physical reality. The same descriptions come back to us from the spiritual world. Everytime people use the same language. OK, it's partly conditioning, this consensus – but only partly. The same descriptions come back to us: a Plain of Nothingness, a region where everything is dead, the Abyss, the Oasis, the One True Path etcetera. Karen, she mentioned one of the most famous: the Path of

Righteousness. "The steep and jagged Path of Right-eousness" is how it is described in the Bible. If my research is correct, however, it is not steep and jagged at all, but smooth and undulating with sharp curves: uncannily like the Log Flume at Alton Towers, in fact. And so it would be more accurate to speak of "the Log Flume of Righteousness".

'Once we have maps for the soul, then we won't be so lost; then, a man may see how long he is likely to endure a state of, say, hopelessness, by knowing its exact pattern or force or topography, and plotting that against time and what he knows of his soul. Maps! That's the stuff! That's the prize!'

He went off and rummaged around in his bag, and came back with a large roll of white card and blue plastic. I helped him clear a space among the plates and empty bottles. He turned the light of the Calor gas lamp up, but seeing how much food was all over the floor, we went up into the peeling-white paint of the pilot-cabin.

The engine was noisy here. The Captain gave us one look and returned to his thoughts which were somewhere at sea outside the black window.

Over Claud's map was a cover sheet of bendy blue-tinted perspex like over an architect's drawings. When he lifted off this cover page, the map looked like a cross between annotated Hubble pictures of Jupiter, and those Conquistador maps with their huge white voids where the Mid-West of America should be. (Entirely accurate as it turned out.)

'Maps! How it all fits together, now we're getting somewhere!' As he pointed, I was surprised how arti-san his small, brown hands were. 'Now look here, the

Valley of Despair. Now everyone knows that on the floor of the Valley of Despair we find the Springs of Hope. But what feeds the Springs of Hope? Well, we also know that close to the Valley of Despair is the Slough of Despond – here. Where does all that slurry from the Slough of Despond go? It doesn't just vanish into thin air, that's for sure. It drains away from the Slough of Despond – through this escarpment slope – to feed the Springs of Hope.' Claud replaced the blue transparent top-sheet. On it, in felt-pen he had indicated the best places to make a Leap of Faith. These fitted neatly over some of the smaller Dykes and Chasms of Doubt on the white card beneath.

Once, when it was just the two of us sitting in deck-chairs up on the roof of the wooden pilot's cabin, I told Claud about a recurrent feeling I had of being 'engulfed'. I nearly didn't tell him, as I was worried that the very act of telling him would make me feel engulfed again. He didn't say anything, merely took off his thick, black-framed glasses and handed them to me. I put them on. Suddenly, I was looking through wrong-way-round binoculars. I looked down at sea and boat as if from a crow's nest. About a hundred yards away, it seemed, I could just make out a grin on Claud's binless face. Handing them back, I was at first angry with him. All the time I thought I'd been having a face to face conversation, I had, without knowing it, been shouting and gesticulating from a distant horizon. But then I burst out laughing.

Talking to Claud was only sometimes pleasurable, however. His smile after you said something was like he was smiling _at_ rather than _with_. You got the irritating impression that you'd typically correlated with something on a graph, and you expected to crop up in some future monograph, entitled *The Bouncy Castle of Oblivion*, or something. There were no hmm-mms or yeahs in Claud's conversation, either. After you'd finished talking there would be a pause. When he spoke, you never knew whether what he was saying was picking up on what you'd said, or whether he had just totally ignored you.

Claud lifted a bulky fishing-weight off one end of the map, which then scrolled up automatically.

'Karen's whole soul's at stake,' I said, 'If she loses the case, then all that faith in human nature, all that doing the right thing . . . It'll change *who she is*.'

There was a pause (while my words crossed the un-bridgeable distance, perhaps).

'Ghetto morale is all about bolstering,' said he. 'Throwing away negative thoughts and pumping yourself with personal propaganda. "Thought", to Buzz, is not rational, but rhetorical. It's self-persuasion by repetition.

'As inner-cities, from Los Angeles to Moscow and here in Britain, retrench into warrior societies, what we've got, historically speaking, is nothing less than the replacement of Greek guilt culture (on which Western civilisation is founded, by the by) with Roman shame culture: the created or conceived self as viable as what we might call the "actual" self. Mark Anthony had a twenty-foot golden statue of himself over his left shoulder. His suicide came about when he failed to live up to this statue, and his killings when others failed to believe in it. Then again, I think Western civilisation has always underestimated how much Roman shame culture still adheres. In suicide, again, for example – how often is the suicide saying: "Well, if I can't be this person (lover, solvent businessman, good guy, winner, free man, adolescent), then I won't be anyone at all."'

'Hmm-mm. Yeah.'

I went back down to the hold, and slung my hammock. Lying back I could see the cabin through the hatch. I saw Claud smooth the map out again. It was a bit eerie him being next to the Captain and among the _Nellie_'s sea-charts and brass box-compass, head down over his own map, plotting another course through black windows.

Next morning was an unexpectedly bright, warm day for late November. T99's rave anthem 'Anasthasia' was playing on the disco-boat's system. From out of nowhere, a flock of swallows appeared. Everyone went up on deck to greet our visitors. Even that old keep-below Kevin joined in. For about the first time on this whole trip, he left the little cabin in the prow where he had been writing his letter to Kenny Rogers, his random notes and memories, making his peace.

'Did you catch the end of my story?' Marlowe asked him.

Everyone was throwing torn-off chunks of buttered baguette to the birds, lobbing Brie and aiming grapes. The swallows swooped away from all these, as if they were missiles that might bring them down. After long trial and error, however, we found that a bowl filled with Ribena or Lucozade brought them right down on to the deck in a noisy clamour. They had no resistance to us picking them up or stroking them. Karen came up from below, packed for her car ride, holding her new suitcase and a spare coat, as well as the three-quarter-length leather jacket she had on. Several of the swallows appeared transfixed by a sparkly Russian cross she was wearing. They perched, entranced, on the back of a chair level with it, then on her lap and shoulder, while she giggled. Suddenly some sombre Smiths came from the system. The swallows scattered. They wheeled away with screeches of bummed-out distress, as did Kevin.

By the time we docked, the temperature had fallen as fast as a thermometer dropped into the sea. It was bitter cold. In the age it seemed to take Polish Joe to bring her around into the trawler harbour (the Captain having turned in), we saw Gina, walking along the mud flats with Monty the dog. She was alone now, having split up with the ineveryway ambiguous Maxine.

The mud flats were all but deserted apart from a family, a couple of kids, and some pensioners. I watched Monty run and stop, run and stop. He bounded in short spurts round the flats and their mini mud-pools, in which he occasionally inspected a pure, white, flexy ghost crab. I was hoping that I was about to witness that moment – if it ever happens – when the once-whipped Blue Cross dog thinks, 'It's been a long time since I was whipped. I may never be whipped again', the furrows on his haunted brow smooth, and his tail wags absent-mindedly. That would have been a good omen.

Looking from aft as we backed out to sea, I watched Karen walk towards the car park. She passed a man in a motorised wheelchair by the war monument. The man, in his thirties, was accompanied by two women with handbags. The wheelchair was equipped with a Hawking-style speech pad and multiple gadgetry.

'Good luck!' we shouted to Karen, as she turned round to wave by Gina's car. 'We'll be back in London by morning. Let us know as soon as you know!'

'I will. Cheerio!' Bib-bib. Karen and Gina drove off.

The war monument was an eighteen-foot, lantern-jawed, cast-iron, greeney-grey Tommy Atkins. A wreath of poppies on the step was covered in clear plastic with white paper underneath. The man in the electric wheelchair could, I noticed, only move his finger and his eyes. He was accompanied by what I took to be his mum and one of her friends. Then, when they weren't looking, he drove his high-tech chair forward over the harbour wall and into the briny. All this was done by the slightest movement of his forefinger, like bidding in an auction.

Kevin and I dived in, but, strapped into a hundred-weight of steel, the man drilled five fathoms down to the bottom of the harbour. Drop. Splash. Gone.

Coming to rest among muffled silt and seventies Littlewoods trolleys, strapped to a chair and duo-decahedrically paralysed, one might, with some confidence, expect to die. But it so happened that, this being Remembrance Day, army frogmen were already swimming about in the murky water, searching for an

IRA bomb under the monument. It so happens that if the human body falls into water below freezing, it can survive for longer.

They brought him to the surface after a good four minutes, not only still alive, but also – we learnt over the cabin radio – without any brain damage. Or rather – with the brain damage he already had *perfectly intact*.

Eleven
TYPHUS IN THE TIME OF CHOLERA _____

Back on dry land now, Kenny. Home again.

Elizabeth Kubler-Ross wrote the splendidly-titled *Death – The Final Stage of Growth*. Working in a hospice with the terminally ill, she noticed that people go through the exact same seven (or is it ten?) phases when they're told they're going to die. I can't remember them all, but it was like – denial first, followed by mad hopes for a cure, then isolation, fury, mourning. The penultimate one is the desire to put your affairs in order. And at last there's being ready, and turning with calm acceptance to face death.

I think there are also distinct phases when you've been chucked.

Can't Believe It's Over

Every throbbing taxi outside, I think: 'Ah, that's the reason she hasn't returned my call. She was so fired-up at the thought of seeing me that she hopped into the first taxi, and here she is, at the door, on the stair, in my arms. "God bless you for wearing those stockings, God *bless* you!"'

The 'If Only' Chimera.

If only, if only . . .

If only she'd been there when I got a laugh at the match. A sunny Paxton End during a quiet spell in the second half. I'd wiped the hot-dog from my face, and joined in the bitter groan of disappointment as 'the cultured right foot' of Klinsman muffed again. Put my cup of tea on the ground between my feet. The stands quiet as the breeze. Why not? I thought. I cupped hands round my mouth and declared: 'Taxi for Klinsman'. A hearty open-air laugh, yeah – even a couple of looks round. How could she not fall in love? I thought.

I Just Can't Get Over You.

There was a time I call 'Before' . . . Two weeks on, this is the first time I've filled the car up with petrol since she left. What a painless thing a petrol-station used to be. A doddle. It used not to swim in a petrol-haze of grief. Today was the first time I've adjusted the clock on the hi-fi since we split up. The clocks have gone forwards an hour, she was in that other time, and now I'll never get her back.

NB: For the next few pages, such points in the writing at which I broke down in tears are indicated by the use of a full-stop.

So, now we begin – wait up – hold on. There, that's much better – oh, no.

Her beige foundation on the sleeve of my white bathrobe.

All this has confirmed the sense that I'll never be

happy. Is that a deep genetic knowledge, deep in the tea-leaf-shaped chromosomes – or just bollocks?

Her car in Archway, her car in Finsbury Park. Every time I see a car like hers it hurts. Pulse soars, my stomach fills with burning, black, churning adrenal medulla. A yellow Beetle drop-top, just rare enough that it could in fact *be* her car parked up in a side-street in Primrose Hill this morning, covered in moss and twigs (because she hasn't left their love nest for days). Or double-parked in Chalk Farm (double-parked in her haste to run into the bed of her Chalk Farm lover? Did he throw his keys down, laughing – *ahahaha* – from that sash window? Did they land in that privet hedge? Am I fucking mental?).

Is this love? Or proof that I never loved her? Or is it the true love of a sick man – the mentally ill, madly in love? Either way, I wince when I see a yellow Beetle. Her life, that I don't know anything about, with strange addresses. Her car is a relic of a better world: an image of her ubiquity; a blameless version of her; a sexist idea of her: trim and built for fun; and, above all – locked.

The only car in a West Ken street with all the parking space of the first London colour films. Then, it seemed like the technicolour city had just been made. The right number of people, the right number of cars filtering through the new streets according to plan. Everything fresh as the lick of paint on postbox and red bus. There was a filmy colour over things in that other world, a richer texture to life.

Isolation
First Sunday since since she's been gone, since all hell

broke loose, I went down to Boot's in Camden to pick up my Prozac.

Had to cross an anti-vivisection picket. Took a leaflet on my way in so they wouldn't shout at me. (Not now, please. Not today.) While waiting for my scrip by the counter, I read the photostat: an unflattering shot of a beagle, a spectacularly unhappy monkey, a bloated-eye cat that you wouldn't want as a pet. The text was against testing cosmetics on animals – cool, yeah, OK – but they were *also* against medical research on animals. This was mind-boggling to me, as I sat on the orange vinyl chair. The idea that, for the sake of a few experiments on what is, after all, a bit of tucker, someone I love could be saved from dying of cancer; a hand I love to hold might not shrivel and chill with arthritis – they want to stop that . . .

My name was called. I pocketed the disappointingly small bottle they'd dispensed me and stepped out through the automatic door again.

'Don't buy from the butcher's!'

I'd lost so many arguments to her. All the personal tenets I'd thought unshakeable had gone down like creaking tower blocks in a yawn of dust.

I went up to the ringleader, a tall, thin crusty with little braided beaded fussinesses in his hair.

'I can't express to you all just how diametrically opposed I am to what you're saying. I mean, this sounds like a rhetorical figure, but it's not – I really mean this: I would genuinely go into any field and kill every single horse, cow, goat, sheep, dog, cat, rabbit, gerbil, if I honestly believed in my heart for just one moment, just *one moment*, that it might be a bit of a laugh.' By now, I had the fellow's Oxfam lapels in my fists. *'BECAUSE I AM SO BORED AND TIRED OF EVERYTHING SINCE SHE LEFT!!'*

Dropping my head on to his bony vegan shoulder, I sobbed loud and long, in great, wracking heaves and gasps. When I finally ceased and straightened up, my hands were full of small, plastic lapel-badges.

Saturday-night shopping is such a blow to morale. The closed-circuit shots say something to me about my life. No plot, no meaning. Nothing to hold the attention for long, before flashing up another aisle, someone more interesting. The Director rubs home the fact that I'm not the hero of even this low-budget late-nighter with a shot of the back of my head, seen from slightly above and to the side. I queue under a sign that reads EIGHT FRIENDS OR LESS. I've never felt so ugly.

Whose knees don't buckle when it comes to love and loss, though? Near the end of his chapter on love, the great philosopher himself writes:

'Although in other respects we may call ourselves happy, we inwardly know that . . . all that was essentially possible has not been realised. We may try to convince ourselves that we have lost nothing when we have lost all.'

Tina is right, though. I've extracted as much pain as possible from this: right from the point where I started to fall in love with Svetlana. Not the moment I first saw her, but the moment I actually fell in love – which was,

as I recall, round about the time we were splitting
up . . .

For some reason our hotel room had two separate
double beds in it. I must have asked for the 'Death of
Romance' suite. It might have been even worse perhaps though, with only one bed: lying so close yet so
far. I couldn't bear the fact that she couldn't bear to
have me near her ('I don't feel like huggink you'). This
was the worst thing in the world. She wouldn't let me
get in the same bed with her. It's like I couldn't see *her*
in focus because of the misty, steaming red veil of my
needing her to like me. I became desperate to touch
her. And when I finally could, again, I was so gushingly
grateful, so relieved. I had no barriers; I fell in love
totally.

I still haven't had the heart to unpack my bag since
that holiday. Today I unzipped it a little and took a
radioactive peek. Didn't touch or disturb anything.
Lying folded on the top was a T-shirt she bought me.
'Don't Leave Heaven Until You've Been to Paradise',
it says. I daren't even wear it in bed.

'I'm happiest alone,' she said. There was a catch in
her hey-ho voice when she said it. Finally, I glimpsed
'the enormity of what I'd done'. (The tragedy of being
only able to perceive the world through fictional
models, or through an *idea* of it – the tragedy is that
you miss out on the truly revealed beauty, when it happens.)

She had wanted her escape, too. She was tired of
having a self as honed as an athlete's body, a soul that she
had to maintain in a kind of enforced condition, like the
training, concentration and practice on a dewy track at

dawn. I saw how rare it was for her to open her heart and fall in love. Life was too real; she wanted to dance for a bit. She wanted a release from the person who nagged and was stroppy. (She found me!) She didn't want to be that person, and for a while, during our 'honeymoon' weeks, she could be warmer, less formal, more spontaneous, unhusked and – well, I dashed that, didn't I?

I see our honeymoon period in a completely different context. Only now I know how rare it was for this woman to open up, and be gentle and loving like that. What a gift, what a jewel – and I let it fall in the dirt.

I saw what I'd done to her.

In the days when the people who read self-help books rule the world, be it known that I believed. Even though I was supposed to see this healing curve as just another ride in the Great American Theme-Park of The Self – be it known, however, that I *believed*. Let the joggers in the germ-free parks of that self-help Utopia know that I believed. May they roller-skate past a statue of me with my thumbs up, (all statues are thumbs up on Alfalfa One). Tell them that I, though British and sceptical, embraced the positive seven-step progression: denial, mad hopes for a cure, putting my affairs in order – it's just the same. And now at last I'm ready, and turn with calm acceptance to face death.

The unbearable shiteness of being. Friends say: 'You've got to stop seeing her as this wonderful being, and thinking that without her your life is just this empty, meaningless crock of shit.' Problem is, she is a wonderful being, and before her life was this empty, meaningless crock of shit. Only now I've got a broken heart, too. They say, 'stop feeling sorry for yourself,' but if I only had their resilience I'd have been dead years ago.

Billy Hurley ushered me into his kitchen and gestured me to a chair as if I'd got there just in time for something grand that was about to start. 'Sit down, sit down, heh-heh, sit down.' His new smile had to work against all the heavy rolls of his sagging face. His smile was a balsa-wood support holding up a collapsed house – it looked like a temporary measure. He sat down with his joints creaking and gave a satisfied '*AAH*'. He grinned at me. There was all this energy dancing about in front of his face that didn't have anywhere to go. I felt worried that if nothing changed in the actual structure of his life, he'd go back to how he was. About a week after this visit he broke his leg on a motorbike, attempting to leap the Devon-Somerset border. And now I know in my bones that Buzz will walk free.

I could say, yes I know I'm gonna be better again; but I also know this feeling is gonna be back here again. And when it's back, it feels like it never went away, like winter in Kiev.

Yours,
Kevin McStay

208

Twelve
REPLY _____

Dear Mr McStay,

I have read your unusual letter. I regret to inform you, however, that it was not I, but Charlie Rich, who recorded 'If You Happen To See The Most Beautiful Girl In The World'. This is a frequent mistake, which, I find, is becoming more tiresome with time.

Yours sincerely,
Kenny Rogers.

Thirteen
JUDGEMENT DAY _____

'Have you reached a unaninimous decision?'

'No.'

'Do you have a majority decision?'

'It's nine-to-three for the Crown.'

'I would like a unanimous decision, but I can accept a majority decision of ten. I will give you more time to attempt to reach a verdict one way or the other. The court is adjourned.'

Karen went to a pay-phone in the corridor. It had sometimes annoyed her the way friends easily assumed that Buzz would go down, but now she needed to hear an outsider's simple conviction in the victory of right over wrong. She only had one fifty-pence piece: who would definitely be in? Who never went out? She made a call and let it ring while she watched the rest of the court empty out into the corridor. Suddenly she realised what would happen if Buzz was found not guilty. 'Oh my God,' she thought, 'he'll just walk out the court by the same exit we all use.' She'd spent two years, during which time not one day had passed without her thinking about this day – and yet in all that time this new and quite horrendous thought had never occurred to her.

DC Jones walked by. 'Oh no,' she said to him, dropping the phone to her neck a moment, 'I've just realised – he'll be a free person in the eyes of the law and everything! Fucking hell! You know, people who are accused should have to go out by a different exit! I mean, I mean . . .'

_____

[MEMO TO MR SCORSESE]

A PHONE RINGING IN AN EMPTY, KNACKERED FLAT (YOU CAN DO ONE OF YOUR CAMERA-GOING-DOWN-CORRIDOR SHOTS – AS, PARADOXICALLY, THE PHONE GETS LOUDER THE FURTHER AWAY WE GET, RIGHT? HEH-HEH, YOU OLD TRICKSTER, MART). A BEE BUZZES AND SETTLES ON THE THICK, STILL SURFACE OF A BATHTUB FULL OF BLOOD. IN THE NOW-COLD BLOOD-BATH LIES THE BLANCHED BODY OF A NAKED YOUNG MAN. SLASHED WRISTS. ON THE FLOOR IS SOME JAGGED GLASS. HIS FACE IS ALL MARBLE REPOSE. BETWEEN HIS KNEES A PLASTIC BART SIMPSON BUBBLE-BATH CONTAINER FLOATS FACE-DOWN IN THE BLOOD. HEAVY BUMMER, DUDE.

PHONE GETS LOUDER.

FROM SOMEWHERE INSIDE THE NAKED
MAN'S COMA COMES A GROAN. A LITTLE
LATER HE STRUGGLES OUT THE BATH.
FALLS, BUT NOT QUITE DOWN. SMEAR-
SLIDES AND STAGGERS ALONG THE
CORRIDOR. (YOUR CAMERA BACKING
AWAY DEFERENTIALLY, RIGHT? HEH-HEH,
I KNEW IT.)

PAINFULLY HE REACHES HIS
DEVASTATED ARM OUT FOR THE
WALLPHONE.

NAKED MAN: Hello? . . . nine to three . . . Oh, I'm
sure you'll win . . . Look, er, Karen, can I phone you
back? Only I've just got out the bath and I'm
dripping everywhere . . . All right, good luck!

HE LETS THE PHONE FALL AND IT BANGS
AGAINST THE WALL A COUPLE OF TIMES.

NAKED MAN: Breakfast!

HE REACHES UP TO A PEELING FORMICA
WOOD-LOOK CUPBOARD. HIS HAND
NEVER QUITE MAKES IT, BUT ENDS UP
CURLING A GRACEFUL ARC, LIKE WAVING
TO FRIENDS IN NEAR-DEATH DREAMS, AS
HE FALLS DOWN DEAD.

_____

Past the Crown Court's white-marbled corridor, in a large atrium with tables, sat DC Jones.

'Now you can tell me about Buzz's previous,' said Karen, as she sat down to join him.

DC Jones let out long breath. 'He burgled and raped an old lady.'

'Oh god,' said Karen.

'That's when I was involved with him before. Except – ' said DC Jones, toying with the torn sugar sachet in his saucer, ' – she was too ashamed to go to court and say she'd been raped – you know, in front of her family and everyone – so we only got him for assault and battery us well as the robbery . . . *Two weeks* scrambling on the Isle of Wight, instead of *three*!'

Within two hours came word that the jury were ready. The trial had been in court no. 11, but for the verdict everyone now filed into no. 4. This was a much longer room with the judge and the now-empty witness box at one end, the public gallery and the defendant right at the other.

Karen sat in the public gallery. There were only twenty-two places. By chance she ended up at the end of her pew. On the other side of clear perspex was Buzz. They were side by side. He was staring straight at the judge.

The jury filed in. Karen noticed that the forewoman looked really nervous and her heart sank. She was about twenty-six and black. She was overweight but it suited her; she carried it well in her Jaeger suit. She had medium-brown skin with hair in a twenties flapper-girl bob.

'Have you reached a decision?'

'Yes.'

The forewoman seemed to have got stage-fright and was staring into thin air.

'How do you find the defendant?'

There was a pause while the forewoman snapped out of her stage-fright. When she announced the verdict she said it hastily, correcting the error of her silence. After all this long trial and two-year hell, it strangely came out sounding like she had come to her senses with innocent surprise, to find herself in the middle of a courtroom, and blurted out the first thing that came to mind:

'Guilty.'

A shriek: cheering and clapping. Karen looked at Buzz through the perspex divide. From right by his side she saw his face fall.

'Will the prosecution read out those of the prisoner's previous convictions which the Crown would like to be taken into consideration.'

The prosecution rose with a sheet of paper in his hand. 'The Crown would like the following offences to be taken into consideration in the sentencing of Andrew Campbell: that on the twelfth of March [. . .] the prisoner was convicted of the armed robbery of a Post Office with threat to kill, and the grievous wounding with a knife of a woman bystander as he made good his escape; that on the third of November [. . .] he raided a building society with a knife and threatened to kill; the grievous bodily harm with a knife in the same month of Troy Prendergrass; that on the second of February [. . .] he committed an aggravated burglary in which he assaulted the female pensioner whose private residence it was; and, finally, the Crown would also like the court to consider that the murder of Glen Johns was committed while Andrew Campbell was on the run, having escaped while serving his sentence for this last-named offence.'

A tall, thin black woman on the back row of the jury burst into tears. These details were all new to them. They had been kept from the jury so as not to prejudice them. While hourly slurs had been heaped upon Karen's head – liar, slut, policeman's whore, insane attention-seeker – these reflections on Buzz's character were inadmissable. The law says that while a man may have raped an old woman in the past – hey, that was a one-off, you know? I mean it's not as if he's a raping-old-ladies _kind of a guy_. Hell, you know how it is: you have a few drinks, you rob a flat, and, well, we all know what the sight of an octogenarian eating some tinned soup does to a man . . . But, that was then, this is now, right?

The law has no option but to believe in the possibility of the absolute transcendence of the past, but the statute, as it stands, believes in a re-invention of self such as only Billy Hurley or David Bowie have ever managed.

Fourteen
OLD SOLDIERS ─────────────

After his motorbike crash, Billy Hurley did start drinking again, but he never went right back to the bottle like before. He'd met a man in hospital called Johnny with a liver complaint. It turned out that years ago they'd had people in common, people from before the war who Billy could remember. And, during the war – before Billy's capture – there were a couple of times when they must have been within yards of each other, Johnny claimed. (Here, Billy just nodded.)

Billy has joined Johnny's petanque team. He has (despite the booze) a good hand with the bowls, a good eye too. The team recently won an All-London cup, and are going to France this month for a competition there. 'Well,' Billy says these days, 'it's better than a kick up the jacksey, isn't it?'

Fifteen
THE PARTY ⎯⎯⎯⎯⎯⎯⎯⎯

Over the excited chatter of Yates's Wine Lodge, the usher was saying to Jimmy Beck, 'This is very rare, you know, everybody coming to the after-trial party like this. The clerk of the court, the jury, the witnesses, the police, everyone.'

The victim's family bought everyone champagne. The first person Karen went up to was the tall, thin black juror who'd started crying when she heard his previous.

'Well done. You made the right decision, you really did,' she said, but the woman looked at her gravely, her eyebrows raised.

'No. I didn't.' The woman knew she'd made a mistake. Her tone of voice was almost like she wanted Karen to have a go at her, to make her feel less guilty.

Karen was brimming with so much joy that she bore the woman no ill-will. How brave of her, she thought, to come here. 'Well, luckily, it didn't matter in the end.'

The only member of the jury who didn't show up at the party was the middle-aged, bearded black electrician who had sat with a snarl on his face throughout. He was the other not-guilty; both knew they had made a mistake. She could show her face now, because her motive had been sound though her decision had been wrong. He could not show his face – not because his decision had been wrong, but because his motive had been bad. And not just his – a retired, white farmer's decision had been right but his motive had also been wrong. Even though Buzz was guilty, the farmer's guilty verdict had been motivated by racial prejudice.

In the jury debate, the thin black woman had at times thought Buzz guilty, and at times innocent. But what swayed her finally was a tone she heard every now and then from the farmer: a tone of elation, of vindication, the primitive relief when archetype and actual seem to match. She heard a certain glee in how neatly the evidence of this particular case reinforced his long-held idea. Or if not glee, it was an alacrity of conviction. And so she was, in fact, right, when she thought that arguing for Buzz's innocence was arguing against prejudice.

Karen was always to think of this party as the best in her life, and chiefly because it was such a cross-section. She was talking to a man with steel-rimmed glasses and wavy, reddy-grey hair who had a job in the accounts department of the local authority. He had a high, pinched voice, which was now speaking in tones of revelation: 'Ooo, that one, you know, the one that had been done for possession and everything else. Taking drugs is one thing, isn't it, but when somebody gets killed it's quite another thing, isn't it, altogether? I think everyone here – well, it's changed a lot of people's lives. I mean a lot of these kids, yes, they take drugs, but they do care, they do care about . . . there's a moral sense, if you like.'

Glen's mother had earlier fixed Karen a look in the eye that was pregnant with meaning. They had been at a distance from each other then, with hands to be shaken and people to be kissed. She was smaller than Karen, with a plump figure. She wore a dark purple twin-set with large gold buttons and a navy blue border all round its edges. Her age showed most in her neck and manicured hands – their skin weathered, full fifty years old – and the site of glamorous jewellery. Now they were face to face, and Karen smelt the woman's strong but pleasant Opium.

'Thank you. I know what you went through.' She laid the lightest of touches on Karen's hand, which almost startled her as they were eye-to-eye.

'Well, I just thought, you know, suppose it had been my sister . . .'

'I really feel that because of what happened through this trial, my son didn't die in vain.' Glen's mum spoke in an even, measured way that Karen guessed was not habitual with her, but to do with fate and occasion. And it wasn't self-conscious or affected; Glen's mum was in that state where there is a sense of pared-downness to what is available to you to say, and where each word feels more weighty than usual. There is an Old Testament word which translates as 'utterance', for when you don't know what you're about to say but the sense feels certain and guided.

Glen's mum continued: 'The way that it's brought everyone together from all different walks of life, and they way people have shown that, when it came down to it, they were prepared to stand up after all for all those fine things in the actual . . . When you watch a film, you're on the side of the people who stand up for all the fine, noble things . . . but when it came down to it, it showed that people would actually do that thing.'

It being the only thing she could think of to do, Karen threw her arms around the older woman. While they embraced Karen could feel the woman's broad body sliding in its underslip. They broke off, Karen grinning at the mother, the mother grinning back, then looking down to dab the inner corner of her eye with her ring finger, shoring up the thick blue eye-shadow.

After Yates's, they moved on to a late pub with a lock-in. A just-this-once nod from DC Jones re-assured the apprehensive barkeep.

Here Karen had the same sense of not-quite-knowing-where-her-party-ended-and-the-others-began that she'd had at Yates's. It was partly the we-are-family feeling of being pissed, but it was something else as well.

In the toilets she chatted on good terms with a woman she didn't know. Coming back from the ladies', she had to wait while a cute-looking boy crouched down to line up an endgame pool shot. The cueball hardly grazed the ball he was aiming at (which didn't move).

'You mean I waited just for *that*?' she said to him. Someone else might have said the same words and been told to fuck off. The young man grinned and nodded as he handed the cue across the table to his opponent.

A second wave arrived. Many of the jurors had

phoned their families when they had been in Yates's. One of these new arrivals – the usher's wife – had come with a big tupperware box filled with eats and treats. In unwrinkled Bacofoil were breaded chicken bites, canapés, cocktail sausages, cheese and pine-apples on cocktail sticks, tortilla chips, and dips. The landlord cleared a table and wiped it down with a 'you notice I'm clearing a table and wiping it down, Officer' look to DC Jones, who pretended not to notice. The landlord helped spread the food out on paper plates.

DC Jones was with the same two plain-clothes officers that had met Karen at the station. 'Here she is,' he said, putting an arm round her shoulders and squeezing her off the ground. 'Hiya champ!' He kissed her on the cheek and put her down on her feet again. She mimed being more dizzy than she was.

He was more grateful than he showed. On the night of the murder he had meant to have picked Buzz up. He'd heard he was going to be in the Rose Cottage that night from an anonymous call-box tip-off. The young male caller knew his name and had a soft down-cast voice. He'd breathed irregularly, as if in pain. At the time it hadn't seemed like a big moral decision. But since then, it had. He felt guilty for the night when he should have done one thing but did something else in-stead, and someone died as a result of his leisurely choice. It wasn't as if he'd gone to a strip bar or any-thing – he'd been working, but had he chosen the easier of two tasks? he asked himself.

The forewoman was being comforted by another juror. As she mopped up some tears with a serviette, she leant across, tapped Karen on the shoulder and said, 'Oh, 'iya!'

'Hi . . . You didn't think he was innocent, did you?' asked Karen, wondering why she was crying.

'Oh no, I knew he was a cunt,' said the woman, off-handedly. 'I'm Carlene; hi Karen.'

'Hi.'

'My brother was killed in a stabbing ten years ago.'

'Oh, I'm sorry. Was it a murder?'

'Nah, just two teenagers fighting, you know. I've had to face up to a lot of things I'd put on the back-boiler, but they don't go away, do they?'

Glen's brother came by and refilled their empty champagne glasses in a mock-Jeeves way. The forewoman poured some on the floor in remembrance, took a swig herself, and said, 'I'd never really contemplated just how awful Roy's death must have been. But in court, when I listened to the pathologist talking about the murder victim, and then they showed us big blow-ups of the mortuary pictures and everything else, I thought this is what happened to my brother, that that is what he went through, and I realised that he must have been in so much pain.'

Karen, Theresa, Carlene, Jimmy Beck, DC Jones and another cop walked back through light rain to the minicab office. Behind them were another gaggle of jurors and friends who would occasionally call something out to the leading group.

Karen drifted out of the conversation and had a delicious moment of being alone with her own thoughts. She stayed outside in the cool, fine drizzle while everyone else went inside the plywood office.

She stood under the silent yellow siren light of the mini-cab office, and watched as a night train crept over the bridge. Slowly every carriage clink-clink-clinked past, the lights all on and not a single passenger in the whole train. In this new world you had only, it seemed to her, to scratch a little below the surface to find the extraordinary in everyone's life. The sense she had had on the train to Stoke, that awareness of being somehow cut off from everyone else, had not only gone, the opposite and counter feeling was much stronger than it had ever been before.

It was 2 a.m. when Karen and Gina got home. She danced around the room with a wine glass in her hand. 'Let's Stay Together'.

'It's like the only real party I've ever been to, where there was something real to celebrate,' she was saying, while Gina built a spliff on the floor. 'Everybody was there and talking in a way that you, er, never get with strangers. This whole thing brought a whole load of strangers with, er, different opinions, different lives and everything else into this, like – it seemed like, you know, almost their whole – it was just like maybe this was, you know, the point where, you know – *life all makes sense*. All these little pieces are joined together and suddenly it was all quite clear; you know people's lives weren't accidents. Most of the people were really *nice* . . . It was amazing how many nice people, genuine people, were there, and they really cared. . . . I dunno . . . I mean, it's just one of those things, isn't it?'

223